Little Sally thought,
Am I going crazy?

She thought, How does a crazy person *know* she's going crazy?

Fact: I adored my husband. We came home from the party and made love and went to sleep.

Question: Did I wake up, load the gun and shoot my husband in the face? What would have been my motive?

And then she thought, Fact: A crazy person doesn't *need* a motive!

Robert B. Gillespie

is also the author
of Raven House Mystery #19

The Crossword Mystery

*"Chilling whodunit plot…
fiendishly clever murder
mystery."* —Quality

She starved to death
in the midst of plenty.

But the "plenty" was on the other
side of a locked door.

Someone had gone to great pains to
confine her in the soundproof room.
With no window, with no telephone,
with no way to reach the outside
world, she could only scream for help.

But no one could hear her. There was
no help. And when she attacked the
door with her one weapon, a letter
opener, she succeeded only in
making a few gouge marks.
Succeeded, too, in starving to death.

LITTLE SALLY DOES IT AGAIN

Robert B. Gillespie

A RAVEN HOUSE MYSTERY FROM

WORLDWIDE

TORONTO • LONDON • NEW YORK

Raven House edition published April 1982

Second printing April 1982

ISBN 0-373-63030-1

Printed in Canada

1

SHE COULDN'T HEAR what Walter was saying. He seemed to be pleading with the desk sergeant, acting out an earnest pantomime for the unresponsive cop. The clock on the wall behind the sergeant said 5:39. A tall policeman stood beside her, impersonal as a statue. The other policemen had disappeared through the first doorway on the left, down the hall. Her gaze swung across the hall to a door marked Men's Room. She felt a chill. She said to Walter Keller, "I have to go to the bathroom." He half turned, nodded absently, turned back to the sergeant. She didn't really have to go to the bathroom.

Walter Keller looked weird. His pale orange hair was tousled; he was dressed in a navy blue blazer, dirty white ducks, and bedroom slippers. Under the blazer, a pink-striped pajama top could be seen. Under the hair, his muffin face with raisin eyes was both sunburned and sickly pale; an upturned nose made him look like a benevolent pig strayed from a children's book. Not at all the way a Manhattan corporation lawyer should look.

She waited, wondering, feeling nothing, a fragile figurine.

Commotion at the entrance. Two policemen

brought in a man in rumpled clothes, a lumbering
blond man, his eyes swollen almost completely
shut, a battered polar bear. Straight ahead, Mac.
The desk sergeant looked beyond Walter Keller at
the trio. Sleeping in a doorway on Bell, wouldn't
move on, called us pigs. The sergeant nodded,
switched his gaze back to Walter Keller. The
policemen led the docile hulk past Sally. He had
the smell of a gymnasium, not unpleasant to her.
They took him to the first door on the left. In here.
The hulk didn't move, glared at the doorway. One
of the cops pushed him toward the doorway. The
hulk whirled clumsily, his right arm was raised
and at the end of it was a fist the size of a sandbag.
The back of the fist hit the policeman on the side
of his head, sent him sprawling, slow motion,
halfway back to Sally; the blue hat, sailing farther, struck her foot. The second policeman had
drawn his gun, was crouched, pointing. Sally's
policeman shouted something to him, moved away
from her toward the swaying giant, slowly, making soothing motions, soothing sounds. The
policemen in the room had now appeared in the
doorway, momentarily in stop action. Walter
Keller and the desk sergeant had turned and were
watching. I'm invisible, she said to herself, and
she walked out.

SALLY WAS OUTSIDE on the sidewalk. In the light of
dawn, a few cars and trucks went their solitary
way along Northern Boulevard almost in silence.
To the right lay Savage Point, Great Neck and
eastern Long Island. She turned left, flitted past
the public library, glided diagonally through the

gas station at the corner of Bell Boulevard, out of sight of the 111th Precinct.

She turned into the street paralleling Northern Boulevard, walking swiftly with easy movements away from her destination. She was wearing high heels, which she wore only to parties and to church. Why did she wear them to the police station? Something terrible had happened, and she was wearing the simple blue dress and thin blue sweater with a pink scarf at the neck, her church clothes. Hanging from her shoulder was the air-travel bag she had used on her honeymoon. She knew exactly what was in it—her toothbrush, toothpaste, her warm pajamas and snuggly slippers, two extra panties, a slip, a blouse and skirt rolled up, a roll of Life Savers, and her purse with forty-seven dollars and change.

At 211th Street, she returned to Northern Boulevard. The number twelve Cityline bus had just crossed 210th Street, coming toward her, heading east. Fifteen seconds later she was on the bus and the door had closed. She had no token. She needed the exact fare of fifty cents. She found forty-five cents in her purse. The driver said that was okay.

No one was waiting at the bus stop in front of the library, so the bus rumbled quietly on without stopping, past it and the police station. Policemen were rushing out the front entrance. Five. Two ran to the corner of Northern and Bell to look north and south. The others ran around the corner of 215th to their blue prowl cars. No one looked at the ten-ton bus that rolled past them, going east.

AWARENESS SEEPED BACK SLOWLY, like pain after novocaine. Her feet were cold, covered with muck. She was crouched in the corner of a duck blind with a staved-in bottom marooned in the marsh reeds of Little Neck Bay. She clutched her stomach to make it sit still. The sobs were subsiding. She was Sally Cochran—"Little Sally" the newspapers had called her when she was an Olympic gymnast competing against Olga Korbut and again when she was accused of killing her first husband, Willie Spencer. She shuddered with the cold and mounting memory; she tried to will the numbness back and couldn't. It was 7:00 A.M., the last Sunday in September, and her second husband was dead. *Steve—oh, God!* She forced her mind away from what happened, sending it spiraling backward.

THE DUCK BLIND was one of the first things she had seen when she and Steve Cochran had moved to Savage Point in June, three months ago. It was their first real house, more than big enough for the family they planned. Steve had said, "At least three," and she had said, "We'll see how it goes." Three months went quickly. The fine edge of her gymnast's agility having been dulled by her long stay at Kings County Hospital, running was now her sport; and daily, from the second day on, she ran the two-mile route around Savage Point, which juts like a caried incisor into Little Neck Bay. Marshland borders the point on both sides at its base, and its cusp is capped by a mile-long seawall stretching from the bay around to the shallows of Harper's Cove to the east; massive boulders, piled haphazardly, protect the seawall from battering storms.

And so this was her racetrack; from their house near the western end of Dover Road she sprinted across the base of the point to Harper Road, up Harper past the marsh to the northern tip and down Shore Road past fine homes, including the castlelike Greystone, on past the dock where boat owners boarded the launches for transport to their craft at anchor farther out, and back to the marshland. And there it was, the utterly silly duck blind painted flame red, looking like an abandoned toy in the tall grasses. Tons of storm-tossed debris had come to rest there in the tidal marsh, but only the red duck blind stood out defiantly to catch the passing eye. To Sally, it was strangely endearing.

When she had pointed it out to Steve, his eyes had lighted up. "Gee, I wish I were seven again," he had said, "so we could use it as a clubhouse. We'd be the Swamp Rats and—"

"Marsh, darling. Marsh Rats." Sally had corrected him. "A marsh is higher-class than a swamp." And he had kidded her about turning so soon into a Savage Point snob.

THE BLIND FACED OUTWARD, away from shore and over the tall reeds to Bayside on the other side of the bay. It was a simple rectangular box, with part of the roof and adjacent side open so that the red-eyed hunter could aim high and blow some luckless duck out of the sky. The blind was slightly tilted, the smashed part at the lower end having several inches of mud in it. She huddled at the top end of the board seat, out of sight from shore.

Time to think. Not about Steve, not yet. He's dead, and the police think I killed him just the same as they'd thought I killed Willie Spencer.

Start with Walter Keller. Good-hearted Walter. He
had heard the shot in the middle of the night and
had telephoned—that was the ringing she had
heard in her half-sleep and had mistaken for a post-
traumatic ringing in her ears from the blast—then,
getting no answer, he had padded over from next
door and found her alone with Steve's shattered
body. Ironically, Walter, her kindly volunteer
lawyer and busybody neighbor, had put himself in
the position of being the chief witness against her.
Could he have planned it that way? She pushed the
ungrateful thought away.

The fluttering in her temples, the heaviness of
her eyelids, the cloudiness in her head warned her
that she was sliding into a catatonic state. No!
What's the worst that can happen? Sally, listen,
what's the worst that can happen? A fiasco! Willie
Spencer had said that to her before one of the
Olympic trials. A *fiasco*, and he had smiled as if he
had spoken the funniest word in the English language. She had laughed, too. Nervously. But this
time the fall would not be an ignobly comical one
on her prat. This one could land her trim rear end
in a hospital for the criminal insane, where her
tune-out would be permanent.

She had trapped herself in a cell smaller than a
prison cell. She examined the back of the blind,
saw that a sliver of wood was missing where one
board joined the next. Putting her eye to the opening, she could see an open stretch of Shore Road
where the trees atop the bluff had long ago sick-
ened and died from the blows of winter. A blue
police car rolled quietly by, heading toward the
point, going the wrong way on the one-way street.

The police were looking for her. She imagined the deadpan desk sergeant coming to life, calling off-duty patrolmen back to the station house to join the great womanhunt: "Sally Cochran, female Caucasian, age twenty-six, five foot two, one hundred and ten pounds, dark hair, wearing blue print dress and blue sweater, wanted in the murder of her husband, Stephen Cochran. Unarmed but potentially dangerous. Believed to be in the area of Savage Point."

No, she said, they couldn't possibly have evidence she was in Savage Point. She had headed toward Manhattan on foot. She had stayed on the bus past Savage Point Road and had gone a mile farther to Little Neck Parkway. Those were the only two roads that crossed the Long Island railroad tracks—Savage Point Road, where the police would have been looking for her, and Little Neck Parkway, which crossed the tracks east of Harper's Cove. Only the bus driver had seen her, and the police had probably not yet interrogated him. Shucking her ridiculous party shoes, she had slipped into the marsh at Harper's Cove and had made her way around the point, painfully paralleling her running route through marsh and thicket, from boulder to boulder. Getting past the dock was hairy; since the property was blocked off with anchor fences she had had to wade around them, in sight of the shore. But she was sure no one had seen her. So the police were only guessing.

7:35. A jogger appeared on Shore Road in a gray running suit. She recognized the pastor of the Conservative Reformed Church, John Dantine. The Conservative Reformed was the nearest thing

to an established church in Savage Point. Pastor
John was a handsome man in his mid-thirties who
prided himself on his nifty figure and the cultured
resonance of his voice. Sally had met him several
times on her solitary runs and had told Steve that,
to Pastor John, it was fitness that was next to
godliness. She and Steve had joined the church at
Walter Keller's urging, and she liked the Sunday
services well enough. Besides, the best people of
Savage Point were in the congregation, an important circumstance to Steve, since a young lawyer
must seek the acquaintance of as many people of
substance as possible. Sally said that was hypo-
critical, but Steve with some heat had convinced
her that it wasn't. She forgot his reasoning. It
didn't matter, anyway.

Before Pastor John loped gracefully out of sight
behind the trees, she was sure he was staring at
the duck blind, insinuating his gaze like a child's
finger into the gap at which she had her eye. She
moved away from the hole. Crouched down as she
was, she could see only the host of marsh grass
that besieged her and the blue morning sky above.
No one could see her except from a helicopter and
only from a small sector out over the bay. She
must have been hearing the noise without listening, for with startling suddenness the whirring
sound was overhead, the reeds were bent flat,
shuddering wildly, and the duck blind vibrated,
too embedded in the mud to shift.

Suddenly the whirring was gone and the reeds
straightened, still crouched against new on-
slaughts. Sally went limp. It was a mistake to come
here. She couldn't stand up, much less move

around, for fear of being seen. But where else could she have gone? Nowhere. Not home, probably crawling with cops. Not to Walter Keller's next door. Besides, Walter couldn't possibly harbor a fugitive. He could be disbarred.

She started crying. She hadn't cried since Kings County. Now it all came out, and kept coming. Her sobs seemed to shake the duck blind and cause the reeds to bend away from her.

8:35. The grief storm was over. She squeezed her temples. If you're ever going to escape, she thought, *think tough*. Stomp all over Willie and Steve if you have to, but *think*. The first question stumped her. What possible reason could lead a God-fearing person to murder someone he scarcely knew or didn't know at all? Her shoulders slumped.

WALTER KELLER had brought them to Savage Point. Steven had been Walter's junior partner in Chatham & Pitts, the downtown law firm. When he joined the firm straight out of Columbia Law, he was temporarily assigned to Walter's department, estates and trusts. Walter liked the tall quiet, bespectacled young man and had remained his friend and mentor even after Steve passed the bar and moved over to litigation, where he had wanted to be in the first place. On the surface, Steve seemed too shy a person to be a good trial lawyer. But Sally knew, from her own experience several years later, that he was as good as they came. His total lack of brashness and histrionics became an asset in court where his air of quiet authority and his crisp logical presentation im-

pressed both judge and jury. Walter Keller basked
in his protégé's success.

When Steve married Sally in 1977, Walter took
them both under his wing. He invited them to dinner at his home on Savage Point, where Sally first
met Charlotte and the three Keller kids. Charlotte
was the uncomplicated, hardworking, den-mother
type. The two youngest children were round and
featureless, but the oldest, a boy named Henry,
came through to Sally quite vividly—a gangling kid
of fifteen who had many of the outgoing charac-
teristics of his father but none of the charm. She
sensed he was acting a role, hiding the real Henry,
whoever that was. She didn't like him.

The newly married couple moved into an apartment in Greenwich Village. Sally was attracted by
the spirited, "hang-loose" feel of the area, and
her tattered personality mended to the point
where she could once again walk with loose limbs
and breathe without a catch in her throat. Not
having been on the bars or mat for three years, she
reluctantly relegated gymnastics to the past—
along with Willie Spencer and the bad times—and
took up running, much of it on the abandoned
West Side Drive.

But the Village was not a hospitable place to
Steve. He saw only the purposeless self-
indulgence, the shoddiness of the art, the pot and
the drugs and the ever-present danger of being
mugged. Steve was not at all like the effervescent
Willie, who had raised her to greater heights but
had never satisfied her need for a firm footing
underneath. Steve was gentle, considerate of her
and after the two would wing smoothly in the air,

they would land lightly on solid ground. Easy replaced uneasy, and her love for Steve increased as her emotional wounds healed.

Walter preached Savage Point to them with missionary zeal and, after each sermonette, Sally would say, "Sounds great." Steve knew two other people who lived there and who, he said, "praised it with faint damns." One, Barney Harper, was some sort of a relative of Steve's, a second cousin, he thought. Barney was an educated man who chose to work at his boatyard, dressed roughly with speech to match. He and Steve had never been close. They seldom talked to each other—in fact, only on the rare occasions when Steve was visiting his mother in Mamaroneck and Barney happened to be on the phone with her. In their last phone conversation, for want of anything else to talk about, Steve asked Barney what sort of a place Savage Point was to live in. Barney replied in a sarcastic voice, "Oh, it's just great. It's the people in it who make it a middle-class slum."

Steve grimaced at Sally, and asked, "What's wrong with the people?"

"Hypocrites, phonies and stuffed shirts."

"What about Walter Keller?"

"The same. In spades."

Steve thanked him, and that was that. He related to Sally and his mother what Barney had said, obviously expecting them to find it funny. Sally remembered the look on Mrs. Cochran's face. It was a face drawn by a cartoonist, the round circle of her nose inside the round circle of her head, the squiggles on the cheeks indicating red blotches. Ordinarily, a merry-looking face that may have been pretty at one time. But the eyes now were baleful, and the corners of the mouth were drawn down in an inverted U. She said to her son, "Don't go near Savage Point. Do you hear me, Stephen Cochran? Stay away from Savage Point."

"You make it sound haunted, Bess."

"It *is* haunted."

"You make it sound evil."

She glared at him a moment longer. "No, not evil, Stevie, but you heard what your cousin Barney said. Listen, you have the whole world to live in. Why pick on Savage Point?"

Steve, who was relentless at cross-examination in a court of law, couldn't bring himself to pursue the issue with his mother. To his mild questions, she said, "There's nothing more to know. Just take my word for it."

The other acquaintance of Steve's who lived in Savage Point was Johnny DiGiorgio, or Johnny Dee, as he was known in his business, the Beneficial Carting Company. Beneficial had been a client of Chatham & Pitts for contracts and other routine legal matters. When Johnny Dee was indicted for extortion, along with nine others in the city, the partners had second thoughts about their client, but they reluctantly agreed to have the firm represent him in the matter, provided Steve handled it and kept them out of it.

DiGiorgio and his family lived in one of the expensive bay-front houses on the old Cotton property at the western end of Dover Road. When Steve asked him about Savage Point, Johnny replied, "It's a nice place to live, but I wouldn't want to visit there. The people are too superior for me. They can tell by looking at you how superior they are. Let me put it this way, each one thinks he's King Shit. Okay? And any wop from Brooklyn is an outsider. Okay?"

Okay.

DiGiorgio squinted at Steve as if sizing him up. "But you, Cochran, you'd get along okay, just fine, no offense intended."

"None taken."

In March, Walter Keller had barged into Steve's office in high glee and literally forced Steve, with a strong paternal arm on the shoulder, to go with him to Savage Point—in the middle of a workday! Sally had met them at Penn Station a minute before the 12:20. The Kellers lived near the western end of Dover Road, less than a block from where it came to a dead end at the Cotton Estates and the Alley Creek marshland. The house fronted on Dover Road leaving about half an acre of backyard that ended at a dirt road and a small tract of unimproved woodland beyond. But here was the wonderful thing—the house next door was for sale and a steal at ninety thousand dollars. Grab it, advised Walter. Sally and Steve didn't have that kind of money, but Walter arranged everything. He introduced them to the real-estate agent, Virginia Goldsboro, a big outdoorsy woman who could have been a horsewoman if there were any stables nearby. Walter and Virginia handled the mortgage—at eight-and-a-half percent—the title search—interesting that this ninety thousand dollar steal went for only sixteen thousand dollars twenty years ago—and the rest of the paperwork.

The Cochrans moved in in the middle of June.

Just at the start of the mosquito season. Walter hadn't told them about the mosquitoes. Unless they bathed in insect repellent, the backyard was useless to them for three months. Only last week they had their first uninterrupted cookout, which ended early because of the chill air.

"GODDAMN!" The muttered curse came from nearby, sending a shockwave of fear through her. She put her eye to the slit. She saw the blue police car parked on Shore Road and the cop standing at the top of the bluff looking down. A moment later, she saw the second cop at the bottom of the bluff at the edge of the marsh, only about a hundred feet away from her. "This son of a bitchin' stuff is all mud!" he called to the one at the top.

"You're not afraid of a little mud, are you, Jack?"

"I heard there's snakes in there, and I don't go where there's snakes. No way."

"Orders are orders. Check any place where the loony dame could be hiding. She could be hiding out there."

"The hell you say."

The shock of finding them suddenly so close to her gave way to a calming fatalism that was either great good sense, since there wasn't a blessed thing she could do about it, or the first downward step in a return to catatonia. Loony. Maybe she was. She sat back in the corner to consider, soberly, the possibility that she was indeed a murderous lunatic. The question immediately became a sophomoric trap. How can a crazy person know that she's crazy? Answer: by looking at the illogicality of her actions and logically deducing that only a certified nut would act that way. But can an illogical person think logically?

Facts. Steve was shot in the middle of the night with a shotgun. He was in bed beside her, presumably asleep. The shotgun was his own, a welcome-to-Savage Point gift from Walter Keller. Keller again. Steve had never used it. Actually, he didn't like it, but he hung it over the mantel because it went nicely with the pair of hand-carved decoys that they had bought in the Hamptons.

Facts. The gun horrified her. She had refused to touch it. She loved her husband. They had not had a quarrel last night. On the contrary, they had made love. They'd come home from the Kellers' party at 11:30. She was exhausted by the party but still too keyed up to sleep. She took a glass of milk and told Steve she was going to take a sleeping pill. Steve said he had a better idea. So they made love. Then she took the pill.

Question. Could she picture herself coming out of her sleep at three or four in the morning, getting up, going down to the living room, taking down the gun, finding shells God knows where, returning to the bedroom, shooting the man she loved and making a bloody mess of his strong, darling, intelligent, lovely face?

Facts. The blast woke her up. From what? A deep Seconal sleep? Or from a psychopathic trance in which she did the above? She was aware of movement at the door, but she may have imagined it. The room was pitch black. She thought she was still asleep. Her hand touched something warm and wet. Maybe she heard a faint noise from

Steve, maybe not. She groped for the light on the
bedside table. What had been Steve looked like
something in a butcher's slop bucket. The gun was
on the foot of the bed. She kicked it off in horror.
She moved away from Steve until she was in the
corner of the room; she slid down to the floor and
started whimpering.

She was sure. She didn't kill Steve. A burglar,
then. No, she remembered something else. She
was climbing out of sleep through blankets of
darkness, and the thing that was in her hands,
metal and wood, for just a fleeting moment was,
she was sure of it now, the hellish shotgun. Maybe
there were other hands, she couldn't say for sure.
But a burglar would not have known about Little
Sally. No, someone had killed Steve and had
deliberately fixed the evidence to point to her.
Motive? A crazy person doesn't need a motive.

Her tense muscles were becoming painful. All
she had to do was stand up and show herself. Anything would be better than cowering here, helpless, despairing. And maybe they'd really try to
find the murderer. But she knew they wouldn't.
Not when they already had the killer, some poor
kooky woman who had a thing about husbands.

"I don't see anybody out there. Do you see anybody out there?"

"No, I don't see anybody out there."

"Neither do I. Let's go." The policeman turned
and clambered up the bluff. . . .

9:30. THE DAY WAS WARMING UP. The sun was high
in the east. She ached to move into the sunlight
but didn't dare. Her little red cell was closing in on

her and the reeds pushed closer, menacingly. There had been a moment at the party last night when she found herself in a knot of six or seven guests and the same feeling of panic had come over her. She closed her eyes, as her thoughts went back to the party. Nearly everyone she knew on Savage Point had been there and, unless Steve had indeed been killed by a stranger—or a mad wife—his killer may have been one of the party guests. She tried to picture them, one by one, even though the whole evening was a hopeless blur in her mind.

Walter Keller called it the last cookout of summer. The guests stood in murmuring groups in the living room, observing an unspoken ritual. When you had chatted for fifteen minutes or so with Pastor John and his milkmaid wife, Emma, for instance, and the small talk was becoming forced, you simply said, "I think I'll freshen my drink," went to the bar in a corner of the living room, and returned to another group. In this way, you got to speak to everyone there.

Stop. Picture the Reverend John Dantine and his gentle blond wife, Sally told herself. He is handsome and vain, with a carefully nurtured dramatic presence and the worldliness of a Jesuit. Steve's pastor, Steve's executioner? Nonsense, on the face of it. And Emma, awed by her husband and nearly everyone else, could never, never sight down the barrel of a shotgun to take a life.

Steve and Sally were the informal guests of honor. Though they had met some of the people in the course of the summer, Walter Keller's party

was, in a sense, their debut into Savage Point
society. Indeed the leading lights were there, including several of the Savages; and the handsome
young Cochrans were introduced to them.

She found herself in the enveloping embrace of
a towering man with a square face and the thick
rectangular body of a football guard. "Ah, my
lovely long-distance runner, Sally Cochran! I've
been wanting to do this for three months! But I
couldn't catch up to you!" The voice boomed in
her ear and boomed through the house. Sally
noticed a small woman behind him who was wincing in embarrassment as the voice thundered on.
"I think you and I are about to start an affair!
Don't tell my wife!" Dr. Everett Smith spoke in
exclamations that must have jarred the seismo-
graph at Fordham University. His eyes twinkling
eagerly, his face flushed with jollity, even his gray
hair, slicked back, proclaimed it was time for fun
and games, make way for the life of the party.

Though she knew everyone called him Boomer,
she felt helpless in his grip, painfully intimidated,
resentful, and she replied demurely, "Thank you,
Dr. Smith."

"Hey, she called me Dr. Smith!" he said to the
room. He turned back to her, and she could see
that her mild rebuff had hurt him. "Bless you!" he
said, and released her. He sprang at Virginia
Goldsboro, put his arms around her and pretended
to cry on her shoulder. Virginia was as tall as he
but not as thick-bodied. "The lady doesn't like me!
She called me Dr. Smith!"

Virginia patted him in mock sympathy. "There,
there, Boomer," she said loudly, "Mrs. Cochran

was only being respectful. I think we should all call you Dr. Smith.'' Boomer wailed.

The small woman who had cringed behind him said to Sally, "Don't mind him, dear, he means it as a compliment." A little of her highball spilled on her hand. "He compliments all the women all the time.... Someone filled this too high. I think I better drink a bit of it.'' Walter Keller came over and introduced her as Boomer Smith's wife, Tish. She was quite tiny, about Sally's height and weight but infinitely more fragile. She must have been a beautiful woman thirty years ago, Sally thought.

Picture Boomer Smith. The too determined extra-vert, surely a wearer of lampshades and ladies' hats for comic effect, he seems to be well liked by the others, but to Sally he is a mad bull devoid of tender emotions, potentially capable of any imag-inable form of cruelty. But this is only a first im-pression, she warned herself. Tish Smith is an insubstantial ghost rather than a woman. If she could lift a shotgun, she'd never be able to shoot straight. Cross out Tish Smith.

Sally held a glass of low-calorie ginger ale in her hand. She hadn't touched a drop of alcohol since the frightful night Willie Spencer went off the apartment roof.

Walter Keller and Virginia Goldsboro were chat-ting with Steve. Virginia said, in a voice intended to carry beyond her immediate listeners, "If the builders had their way, they'd fill in the bay and put up Cape Cods. Sally, honey, those wetlands are our lifeline to nature. If we destroy enough of them, we'll wipe human life from the face of the earth.''

Walter and Steve vehemently agreed. Sally asked her about the red duck blind in the marsh. It had belonged to someone in Great Neck, Virginia said, and had been broken loose by one of last fall's storms that had smashed it against the boulders before depositing it in the grasses. ''Doesn't that sort of thing injure the wetlands?'' Sally asked.

Virginia said, ''No, it's biodegradable.''

Sally felt biodegradable. Steve said they had the same ecological problems up in Mamaroneck where his mother lived. Virginia said something like, ''Oh, I didn't know your mother lived in Mamaroneck.'' They carried on about Steve's mother in Mamaroneck. Then Virginia wanted to know how they were enjoying the house she was instrumental in getting them. But she seemed to have turned off. She said, ''I think I'll freshen my drink,'' told Walter and Steve she was perfectly capable of doing it herself, and moved off. . . .

Okay, that's Virginia Goldsboro, the first of the Savages. Sally's recollections of the Savage family were quite confused, since some of them aren't even named Savage, and since Sally was feeling claustrophobic and wasn't paying close attention. She tried to get them straight in her mind, then remembered that Virginia's mother pointed them all out to her a little later at the party. If only I can remember, Sally thought.

Steve and Sally were in a discussion of cesspools with Emma Dantine, Gemma DiGiorgio, and Charlotte Keller. Cesspools were important to the residents of Savage Point. For decades they had fought off all attempts by the city to install sanitary sewers, as part of their rearguard fight against encroachment by high-rise apartments and the ultimate destruction of their peaceful enclave. They loved Savage Point exactly as it was, cesspools and all.

Sally's nerves were tightening, and Steve was trying to guide her toward the back door and fresh air when Sally stumbled over something. "I was wondering when you were going to trip over me," said the woman seated on the sofa. "Don't be embarrassed, it was I who stuck out my cane." Sally had difficulty judging the woman's age. The round face was unseamed except around the mouth, which looked to be a hundred and fifty years old, and around the eyes, which seemed to be the grinningest eyes Sally had ever seen.

"Yes, I'm 'Nosy Alice,'" the woman said. Walter Keller had started toward her earlier with Steve and Sally in tow, but had been waylaid. She was Alice Goldsboro, reigning queen of Savage Point society, seventy-eight and going strong. She took the hands of Sally and Steve and pulled them down. "Come, sit, and tell me all about yourselves." They sat on either side of her, trapped. She said to Sally, "I've seen you running, my dear. You're as swift and graceful as a panther."

"A panther?"

"Well, a gazelle, then. You're a lovely sight to see. Now tell me why you run." She had Sally's hand in both of hers.

"Because jogging seems so dumb—you'd be better off doing isometrics at home."

"Not I." The old lady laughed. "I had a lot of fun putting on this weight. I'm not going to torture myself to take it off." She turned to Steve. "I've been watching you, young man. You look very familiar to me. Have we ever met before?"

"I don't think so, ma'am," Steve replied.

"I'm not your ma'am, and don't call me that. It makes me feel old. Call me Alice, or call me Nosy Alice, if you want. Where do you come from, Stephen Cochran?"

Steve said, "We moved here from Greenwich Village. We had what they call a pad there."

"No, I mean originally. Where were you born and raised?"

Sally couldn't see her eyes because they were gazing steadily at Steve, and, having relinquished Sally's hand, the old woman had captured both of Steve's. He told her he had been raised in Mamaroneck.

The old lady said, "Now don't tell me your mother's name is Elizabeth."

"Something like that," Steve said. "How did you know?"

The old lady chuckled. "Because I'm psychic," she said. "Now I'll tell you about your father. He was the owner of a bar and grill called Paddy's Pub, and he drank hot tea when he was behind the bar."

"Wrong," Steve said. "He was a beer distributor, as far as I know, and he drank his own product. I never met him."

Old Alice patted the back of his hand in triumph.

"There, I was close, wasn't I? A beer distributor instead of a bar and grill." When Sally saw the eyes again, she saw she had been mistaken: the laugh lines were only squint lines, and the eyes were watchful.

"And where were you born, nosy Alice?" Steve asked pleasantly. "And is it true your father was hanged as a horse thief?" Sally held her breath.

But old Alice just chuckled. "I was born right here on Savage Point, and you must be psychic, too, you wicked young man. My father was in real estate. Horse thief, real estate, same difference."

"Then you must be a Savage," Steve said. Walter had told them earlier that she was.

"Sheer clairvoyance," the old woman said. "Yes, James Cotton Savage is my brother. This place was named for him, did you know that?" Steve shook his head. Sally was surprised that the man who had given his name to the place was still living. Typically American, she thought, the land of instant coffee and instant tradition.

The old woman went on, with a show of self-deprecation. "Since you two lovebirds are going to live here, I suppose you ought to get the family straight." She turned her gaze to Virginia, who at the moment was pounding Pastor John on the back and laughing. "You know my daughter, I believe. I'm really quite proud of her. She leads the good fight wherever her services are needed. And Charles. Virginia always called him Cousin Charles, so we do, too. He helps Cotton manage the estate, he's good at signing his name, and he helps Virginia, too, in her work. Do you know

what a gofer is? Well, Cousin Charles is a top-notch
gofer. The best ever.''

Walter Keller was standing in front of them. He
appeared nervous. "I'm glad you all finally got
together," he said with excessive heartiness. "I
promised to introduce Steve to all the firm's clients
on the point. We seem to have a monopoly on the
law business here, Aunt Alice, for which many
thanks." He bowed. "I think he's met them all except one. How's Cotton?''

She squinted up at him. "About the same,
Walter. He has his ups and downs.''

Walter cleared his throat. "Well, if he's in one of
his ups, I thought I might take Steve—and Sally,
too, of course—up to Greystone tomorrow to say
hello to him. Would that be all right?''

The old woman continued to squint up at him. "I
don't know, Walter," she said slowly. "Why don't
you give me a call after church, and we'll see.''

"That'll be just jim-dandy fine, Aunt Alice,"
Walter said.

*So that's the Savage family with the exception of
the ancient patriarch, James Cotton Savage, who
apparently has his "ups and downs" and can't
strictly speaking be a patriarch, for he has no
children. Frowning, Sally tried to get the relation-
ships clear in her mind. Alice Goldsboro, seventy-
eight, is old Cotton Savage's sister, making her
daughter Virginia the old man's niece. But Cousin
Charles was a puzzle to Sally. Since his last name is
Savage, she reasoned, and since he is not Cotton's
son and yet is Virginia's cousin, he must be the son
of some long-deceased brother of Cotton's, whom no
one mentioned. It was all very confusing.*

And not a killer in the lot! A seventy-eight-year-old woman who needs a cane to navigate. The hearty Virginia, in her early forties, who is a part-time real-estate agent and full-time community leader. And Cousin Charles, in his late thirties, who looks like a jolly eunuch. So where does that leave me, Sally wondered. Nowhere. Out in a duck blind, about to fall apart.

Boomer Smith had Johnny DiGiorgio cornered. Boomer was telling him a joke with Italo-ethnic overtones. Boomer's laugh shook the chandelier over the dining table.

Sally heard Johnny Dee say, "That's a good one, Dr. Smith. Now if I can just collect my wife, I think we have to go."

Not much to say about Johnny DiGiorgio, Sally thought. A dark, heavyset man whose rather large nose makes him look virile rather than comic. Sally had heard he has Mafia ties, but she rather likes him. His wife Gemma is scarcely a personality to Sally, nor even a presence. Plump, dark-haired, almost as short as Sally herself, Gemma has a meager store of small talk. When she and Sally found themselves together at the party, they commented on the canapés and the weather, and then they went to freshen their drinks. Certainly Johnny Dee was a ruthless enough man to be a killer. But of Steve? Oh, God!

Sally tugged at Steve, and they made their way, pardoning and excusing through the crowd, to the backyard. Tish Smith was with the Keller kids singing, "Row, row, row your boat." The smell of marijuana was strong in the air. Cousin Charles,

leaning to starboard, was waving his arms as if
leading the chorus. One of the kids detached himself from the group and intercepted them as they
headed to their own backyard, Walter's fifteen-
year-old son, Henry. Sally and Steve had come to
refer to him in private as Sneaky Henry.

"I hope you people had a good time," said
Sneaky Henry, sneaking a look at Sally's bosom.

"Where do you get the pot, Henry?" Steve
asked him.

"Pot? What pot?"

"Oh, come on, I'm getting high just standing
here."

"I don't know what you're talking about,"
Henry said stiffly, and turned away.

In their own yard, Sally said to Steve, "Wow, if
looks could kill—"

COULD IT HAVE BEEN SOMEONE at the party? Steve
didn't have an enemy in the lot. He may have net-
tled Aunt Alice and angered Sneaky Henry, and he
may have bored some of the others—she had to
admit Steve wasn't the most entertaining man in
the world—but to blast a man to kingdom come
just because he bored you?

10:30. To relieve cramped muscles and the con-
stricting claustrophobia, she started a routine of
isometric exercises. She had progressed to a point
where her body was suspended between the
plank seat and the roof when the monotony terminated and she registered that a face was
watching her. The face was in the reeds; it didn't
seem to have a body, just a two-dimensional face
looking at her. She closed her eyes, half believing

the face would disappear. She said, "Go away."

A teenage boy was crouched in the thicket of reeds. The face was long, with a sharply angled nose and chin; black hair that had been plastered down was starting to fall over the forehead. The mouth was partly open, moving as if trying to think of something to say; the large, brown eyes seemed to reflect the misery that was in her.

"It's impolite to stare at people," she said as sternly as she could. "It's an invasion of their privacy. Now please go." The fact that she was discovered had a calming effect. Flight was over, and the loneliness was broken.

The boy looked down at something in his hands, then raised his eyes to hers. "I'm sorry, Mrs. Cochran," he said in a crackling voice. "Can I help?"

"I wish you could. No, I don't think so," she said.

He said, "Is it all right if I leave the bird here for a minute? It's a baby bird. I was going to leave it here and go get it some food." He held out his hands, formed in a cradle.

"Bring it here," she said. "It seems to be all beak and no bird."

"That's the way they are."

He was a skinny kid, about fifteen, in a tan sweater that was too short and blue jeans with ragged edges. He stepped awkwardly over the sill of the duck blind. His feet were bare and muddy.

She said, "Please get in here under cover." It was a repulsive little thing of pinfeathers and open beak.

He said it was a starling. "It wants to be fed. I

found it at the edge of the marsh. It must have fallen from one of the trees and hopped there. I couldn't find the mother." He put it down in the bottom of the blind. It half hopped, half stumbled downhill to the muddy deposit, stopped there with no place to go. Like me, she thought.

"And you're going to feed it?"

He smiled shyly. "I'm gonna try. I've never done it before, but it ought to be simple. What the mother does is find a worm, chew it a little, and shove it in the baby's mouth. I've seen them do that."

"You're going to chew a worm?"

He flashed another smile, and stood up. "Wait, I'll show you. It probably won't work. I'll be back in a minute." He disappeared around the left side.

She was left to look at the ugly little bird.

Suddenly the boy was back, holding a wriggling worm. In disgusted fascination, she watched as he pulled off the back tip of the worm and mashed it between his fingers. "Yecch," she said.

He said, "Birds think they taste good." He spit on the wormy mush, and mashed it some more. "I figure that's like the bird chewing it, but maybe my spit is different from theirs." He picked up the bird, which fluttered, then remained still. He put some of the mush in the bird's beak. "Sorry it's got a little dirt on it," he said to the bird. The bird neither closed its beak nor tried to swallow. The boy pushed it farther into the mouth. "Damn, it's not working," he said. He put the bird down in the mud, wiped his hands on his jeans. "Damn."

She asked, "What's your name?"

He said, "Joey Dee."

"Is Mr. DiGiorgio your father?"

"Yeah, we live right over there." He pointed at the left wall.

"I know," Sally said. "I was there with my husband once. Is that how you knew my name?"

"Well, not exactly. I've seen you around on Dover Road, and I've seen you running around the point. I think you run great." His face reddened, and he looked away.

She took a deep breath. "Do you know that I'm running now?"

He nodded his head, not looking at her.

"How did you find out?" she asked in a small voice.

He turned to her, his eyes flashing anger. "Mr. Keller called my father. And then we heard it on the radio."

She gasped. She hadn't expected the news to be out so soon. "What—what are they saying?"

His mouth flattened as if trying to prevent the words from coming through. "They said you killed Mr. Cochran and then escaped from the police."

She let her head rest against the back wall. She felt empty of feeling. "That's putting it pretty bluntly. Putting the nut in a nutshell, I guess."

He said, "I don't think you did it," glaring at her.

She turned to him with a weak smile. "Do I seem crazy to you, Joey?"

He said, "Well, coming out here was a crazy thing to do. I mean—"

"I know what you mean. But was it crazy or just plain stupid?"

"Pretty dumb. I mean—"

"I know what you mean."

"I didn't mean what I said," he replied quickly.

"I don't think you're crazy, Mrs. Cochran, and I don't think you killed Mr. Cochran."

"Why not?"

"With a shotgun?"

She gave a short nervous laugh. "Well, that settles that, Joey Dee. We both agree I'm not crazy and I didn't kill Steve. Thank you."

"That's all right."

"Which leaves me sitting like a sitting duck in a broken duck blind." Her voice turned to a wail. "I can't move a step without getting arrested."

Joey sat on the edge of the bench, gazing at the sky over the bay. They could hear the helicopter in the distance. "They described you on the radio," he said.

"Yes."

"They said you were wearing a blue dress and had on high heels."

"I was."

"They said you wore your hair pulled back and tied up or something."

She nodded.

He looked at her sideways. "Have you noticed something about Savage Point, Mrs. Cochran? The grown-ups don't walk. They ride. Only the kids walk."

She said, "That's not entirely true, but what are you getting at?"

"They're looking for a grown-up."

She said. "I'm pretty slow, Joey. Are you saying I could make myself look like a kid and—and walk right under their noses?"

He laughed. "Maybe not under their noses."

Hope was once again flickering inside her. "But I'm too old looking."

His cheeks flushing, he said, "You look like you could be seventeen or eighteen, and with your, uh, thin body, uh, you could—"

She pulled at the tan blouse, looked at him questioningly.

"No, a kid wouldn't wear that," he said. He jumped to his feet, crouching under the roof. "If you'll wait a few minutes," he said. "Don't go away." He leaped out into the reeds and in two steps was gone.

His departure made her feel more alone than ever. He would come back, and it didn't much matter whether he brought the police or some worm mush for her to eat.

11:45. Joey Dee was in the duck blind before she was aware of his approach. She didn't know how much she had missed him until she found herself laughing in relief. He was wearing a blue and orange jacket. He plunked a mesh bag, lined with plastic, onto the seat beside her, explaining, "Anybody wonders, I'm looking for clams." He pulled it open. "I walked by your house," he said. "There wasn't any police car there, but I could tell they were inside, so I didn't get any of your clothes.... Anyhow, these ought to fit you, they're too small for me." He pulled out a pair of faded blue jeans, a T-shirt bearing the legend Sailors Have More Fun, white sports socks, a pair of well-scuffed sneakers, sunglasses, a large pair of shears. He also brought out a ham sandwich and a bottle of Coke. Impulsively she hugged him; he pulled away and continued to retreat right out of the duck blind. He said, "Put them on; knock on here when you're finished," touching the left wall, and he disappeared.

Shivering, she changed into the rough jeans and nautical shirt. The jeans were tight in the seat, too long at the ankles. She turned them up. The sneakers were loose on her small feet, but the bulky socks helped to fill them out. With a sense of dangling between two personalities, she knocked. Joey Dee bounded back into the blind.

He looked at her steadily for a moment, all shyness gone, like an artist appraising a work in progress. "We have to do something about the hair," he said. He picked up the shears.

"No!" she cried. Steve had always liked her hair when she unloosed it at night and it fell over her bare shoulders to her waist. To cut it would be like cutting a bond to Steve.

He said, "A lot of the kids let it fly loose."

"Okay, I'll let it fly loose." She undid the ribbon at the back of her neck, shook her head.

"Not that long," he said. "Let me cut it, and I'll show you."

"Not much," she said. "Just a little."

"At the shoulder."

She sighed. "Okay." While he was behind her, she asked, "Where did you learn to cut hair?"

He said, "What's to learn?" She shuddered.

With the earnest thoroughness that she had found to be part of his character, he spent five minutes evening the ends as best he could. "Now," he said, "go like this." He shook his head vigorously and fluffed his hair out to the sides with his fingers.

She looked at herself in the mirror. Her hair stood out like an Afro. She looked dreadful, she thought, but she didn't look much like Sally

Cochran anymore, and maybe she looked like one of those teenagers who always look like they need their hair washed.

"Put these on," he said, handing her the outsize sunglasses.

She looked even less like Sally Cochran. What she saw could have been the magnified head of an insect with enormous eyes. "Weird," she said.

He took off the blue and orange windbreaker and held it out. "Now try this on for size," he said. The bold lettering on the back said Cardozo High School.

The jacket was much too large, the sleeves coming down to her fingertips. "It won't work, Joey," she said in dismay.

"That's the way they wear them. Hold out your arms." He folded the sleeves back to the wrists, pulling away when his hand touched hers. He said, "Stand out there."

"Where they can see me?"

The sun was unexpectedly warm, yet she felt exposed, chilled.

"Good," he said, "you're a junior. Some of the kids try to walk like boys, slouched, swinging their arms, but you're too—" He colored again. "No, just be yourself. The pants are just right."

Standing in clear view of anyone on shore frightened and exhilarated her. "You're a genius, Joey Dee. I'm beginning to feel like the invisible woman." She returned to the bench alongside the boy. "Okay, what now?" she asked. Suddenly free, she felt inadequate, lost, unable to take the first step.

He said, "Find the murderer?"

"But where? Who?" she wailed.

His face reflected her helplessness. "I don't know anything about it. Who'd want to kill Mr. Cochran?"

"Nobody! That's the trouble. Nobody."

He frowned in concentration. "No suspects. No motive. No clues." The big eyes looked at her with disbelief. "My father?"

"What about your father?"

"He was mad at Mr. Cochran."

"Why?"

"Because Mr. Cochran wasn't handling the case right. He wasn't making any noise. He didn't get the judge to lower the bail. He was letting the D.A. get away with murder."

"Murder?"

"You know what I mean. They were railroading him to jail, and Mr. Cochran wasn't doing anything." He added, "That's what my father says."

"And what do you say?"

"My father doesn't kill."

She had known Johnny Dee wasn't happy with Steve's efforts. She knew he was a tough man who had risen from the streets of Brooklyn, possibly through the Mafia. He was accused of breaking legs, but nobody had proved it yet. Actually, she liked him and was a little afraid of him. "Where was your father last night?" she asked.

"Home, in bed."

"You weren't with him all night."

"No, my mother was."

"I can't believe your father killed my husband."

"Neither can I."

"So what do I do now?"

Joey spoke slowly. "My father always says that anything happens on Savage Point the Savage family is behind it. Find out about the Savages."

1:05. SOMEONE WAS WITH BARNEY HARPER. Sally crouched in the launch, now high and dry on wooden frames. The boatyard presented a desolate scene, crowded haphazardly with beached boats. Beside Barney's Jeep was another car, a blue Volvo, that looked familiar. The building was a low ramshackle affair with an office in the center, a long open shed to the right facing the tall reeds and narrow channel of Harper's Cove, and a room to the left that Barney called home.

On the run. She had been on the run for more than seven hours, not running at all, mostly cowering. Peeking over the edge of the launch, she saw the M.D. plates on the Volvo. Dr. Smith. Boomer. She disliked the loud, overbearing man whose eyes had undressed her, and whose stout body she still felt against hers in the smothering bear hug. She'd have to wait until he was gone. Still on the run.

Voices, a man's and a woman's, came across the dirt yard. Barney was coming out of his office with a short, slender woman. He said, "Just don't listen when he gets like that. What you don't hear won't hurt you, honey."

"How can you not listen to Boomer?" the woman asked. Barney and Boomer's wife, Tish, paused in the dirt area.

"Okay then, as I was saying, when he starts after you on the booze, you start after him on the cigarettes. Nag the shit out of him, and maybe he'll shut up." Barney put his arm around her shoulder, grinned down into her face. "You know how to nag, don't you?"

"I guess I can try," she said.

"Come on now, I thought every woman knew how to nag. They learn it at their mother's knee." He continued in a mimicking falsetto, "You a doctor and you still smoke two packs a day, it's suicide that's what it is, you're killing yourself. I don't care whether you kill yourself or not, but think of the children, they're your responsibility, just wait till they're twenty-one and out of college and then you can kill yourself all you want. Cancer! Cancer! Cancer!"

Tish Smith laughed nervously. "Hey, you're good at it. Why don't you come over and nag him for me? Sort of a paraprofessional."

Sally felt embarrassed to be eavesdropping. All was obviously not well in the Smith household, but she didn't want to know about it. The woman abruptly hugged the man and gave him a quick kiss on the cheek. "Oh, Barney, thanks very much," she said. "You always make me feel so much better. I can never repay you."

He pulled away, saying, "Ha, a sexy broad like you doesn't know how to repay a horny old bachelor! I've been wanting to get you in the hayloft all along, you gorgeous thing."

She giggled. "Oh, Barney, you need your eyes examined." The exchange sounded ritualistic, as if the same words had been spoken before. And the forthright pat on the rear end as she moved toward her car, that was ritualistic, too. A booster shot for the female ego.

After the Volvo disappeared around a bend in the rutted road, Barney Harper gazed out over the marsh sniffing like an animal, shook himself and retreated to his doorway, where he turned to take a last look at his domain. Thus, he was looking right at her when Sally vaulted out of the launch and landed lightly on the dirt.

Barney said, "That was a great trick, kid. Now get the hell out of here before I break your neck."

Sally approached uncertainly. Since she hardly knew the man, she had no idea how he would react to a fugitive criminal. "It's me, Cousin Barney," she said in a small voice, pushing her hair back with her hands.

"Sally?" He glanced quickly around, waved her toward the door, "Get in here, you darn fool, before someone sees you." Wanting to walk sedately, she bounded across the open dirt and through the doorway. The office had a large window facing the entrance road and another large one overlooking the marsh.

"Not here." He led her to his bedroom, a small room with a bunk bed in one corner, a twenty-one-inch TV in the opposite corner, a stuffed leather rocking chair, a table and two chairs near the small front window. Bookshelves lined the wall above his bunk. He opened a chest at the foot of the bed, took out an armful of clothes that he threw on the bed. "Okay," he said in his raspy voice, "if they come back, get in here and close the lid. Don't worry, I'll get you out before you suffocate." He glared at her intently. "Got that?" She nodded, knowing that she could never willingly put herself in such a confining place.

He sat her down at the table, placed himself in the other chair closer to the window where he could keep an eye on the outside. They stared at each other. She started to say, "So the police—" He started to say, "You look like—" They both stopped.

"I was going to say, so the police have already been here."

"Twice," he said sourly. "I was going to say, you look like hell. Is there anything I can get you?" He added, "Like a drink or something?"

"No, thank you. Could I freshen up in your bathroom?"

He led her through the office, making her creep past the window, to the shed, in one corner of which was the bathroom. It was neat but not very clean. When she returned via the creeping route, he had a drink in his hand, whiskey on the rocks.

"I felt I needed a drink," he explained, "even though it's not yet the drinking hour. I was just preaching to Tish Smith that she should wait till the cocktail hour, and then she could tank up all she wanted. So here I am going against my own advice and delighted to be doing it. You knew Tish Smith was here? I seem to be the father confessor for all the abused wives of Savage Point. I have arthritis in the shoulder from all the tears that have been shed on it."

"It looks like a strong shoulder," she said.

He said softly, "Tell me about it."

Without meaning to, she told him everything she remembered of the nightmare. His eyes watched her, held her, pulled every horrible moment from her. His face was not really a strong one, almost a soft one, though the skin was leathery from long exposure. The mouth was permanently thin from uttering sarcasms, belying the warmth, humor and sensuality of the eyes. His brown hair, beginning to turn gray, looked like it was combed by fingers only.

Astonished to hear herself telling him things she would have hesitated to say to Steve, she understood the attraction he had for the psychologically battered housewives of the area: he was masculine in a way their citified husbands weren't, he was as well educated as most of them—Brown '61— without bartering his degree for a high-paying job he didn't want, and he seemed to have a sympathetic insight into anything human and hurting.

Yet there had to be darker elements in the man. He was thirty-nine years old and had never married. Steve had told her that. Of course, it could be that the father confessor celebrated black masses in the bunk bed with some of his more sexually frustrated communicants, a form of therapeutic adultery with climactic absolution. Leaving him forever on the outside, alone in this little room. But add that he was a hero to most of the boys of Savage Point. They flocked to his boatyard. He took them on sailing trips.

She had come here to Barney to find out about the Savage family—because Joey had suggested it, because the whole community was a suspect, and because she had no other place to start.

"Okay, the Savage family," Barney said. "They're a bunch of old farts, but do you really think one of them killed Steve?"

"I don't know what to believe."

He made himself another drink, gave Sally a glass of milk, and sat down, half facing the outside window. "First, a little history. The place was called Indian Head because someone thought it looked like the head of an Indian on the map. It was far from Manhattan, cut off by Alley Creek, mostly farmland owned by the Harpers and the Savages. It started to become a residential community around 1900, and, by the time the Depression hit in 1929, there were four hundred houses here, each one built separately, no cookie cutters. The Savages were smarter than the Harpers. The two families sold off their land, bit by bit, but the Harpers pissed the money away while the Savages invested theirs in real estate.

"We now come to James Cotton Savage. He'd made a bundle in the twenties using the family money to build housing developments all over Queens, cheesy but not crappy, if you know what I mean. Well, the Depression knocked the Indian Head families for a loop. Three quarters of them couldn't pay the mortgages on their homes. Some of them couldn't even put food on the table. And they couldn't sell the houses because there was no one to buy them. That's when James Cotton Savage became the great philanthropist. He lost a million dollars himself, but he had several other millions to carry him through. So big-hearted Cotton, he was only thirty-two at the time, got up at the civic association and proposed a deal they couldn't refuse. He would buy their homes from them for five thousand dollars each, he'd let them stay in residence as long as they wanted, and when things eased up he'd sell back their homes for the five thousand dollars plus his out-of-pocket costs. Sounds like a great, charitable thing to do, doesn't it? And maybe he intended it that way, but I don't think so. In the next nine years only about two hundred families were able to buy back their homes, and Cotton Savage wound up owning one hundred beautiful houses and large parcels of land.

"I don't know what all this has to do with Steve, but you asked about the Savage family. By now they're the noble Savages. A few of the Harpers lost their houses to this great benefactor, but it was their own damn fault for having anything to do with him. One of them, incidentally, was Steve's grandmother's family. She was a Harper. That's why I guess it was natural for Steve's father to come back and buy a house here, his family roots being here and all that."

Sally, who had been on the point of drowsing, came awake. "I didn't know Steve's father had lived here," she said. "I knew you were his cousin, and that's all."

"He and I were second cousins, but I'm damned if I'm going to go into our family tree. Too many nuts."

"When did he live here? Was he married to Bess? Did Steve live here? He couldn't have, or he would've known."

"Whoa. Hold it," Barney said. "I was only a little shit at the time, no more than seven or eight, maybe nine. There was just cousin Mike and his wife Betty. They had been married for like eight or nine years. It must have been about 1949. They only lived here for a year or two. Then they moved to Mamaroneck and I hardly ever saw them again. Wait," he said, pointing a finger upward as an indication of a surprise to come. "I'll tell you where they lived. Do you know where that conceited ass of a minister lives? John Dantine?" She nodded uncertainly. "Well, that's the house where cousin Mike lived. When they moved away, Cotton Savage bought it and donated it to the church as a residence for the minister's family.

"That was James Cotton Savage for you. Patron saint of the Conservative Reformed Church. He had married the first minister's daughter. What the hell was that old windbag's name? Edith. She was so pious, she glowed in the dark.

"Anyhow, Cotton Savage was riding high. You know that abomination of a building that's the Savage Point Club? That was the old Savage house before he took some of his waterfront property and built that other abomination he called Greystone like it was a castle, with the British spelling and everything. The only people I know who give names to houses are those who have shacks on the beach and call them things like How My Dune. He considered himself royalty by that time, I guess. And he got himself a yacht, actually a two-masted schooner, the *biggest* yacht this side of J.P. Morgan. Dark gray, like the house, it looked sinister sitting out there in the bay. And he called it— get this—*Lord Jim*. Do you get it? James is his first name." He snickered.

"Well, he had a lot of parties there. In both places. Edith was a shy person or maybe too snooty, so Cotton's hostess most of the time was his sister, Alice. They were a handsome couple and I always thought they should have married each other. Oh, I forgot to tell you. Alice married an alderman's idiot son, George Goldsboro, who was about eight or nine years younger than she."

Sally fidgeted, gripped the table to keep her hands still. She wanted to get back to Steve's connection or lack of it. Joey Dee's ham sandwich was restless in her stomach and the milk was curdling. "Do you have any chicken soup?" she asked.

While he heated the water for her soup, he continued his story. "George must have got it up at least once, because even the Savages don't have immaculate conceptions. So it came to pass that a girl child was born unto them. Let's see, Virginia is three years older than I, so that would make it 1937. Maybe the sight of Virginia turned them off, maybe George wasn't the father after all because Virginia was a big buster right from the start; whatever, there were no more children. Matter of fact, all the men in the family may have been larger than life in all other areas but not between the legs. Old Cotton never had any children, though that may have been Edith's doing. She was too holy to have congress with such a profane thing as . . . well, never mind. And Cotton's brother Ed, he married one of the Smith girls, everywhere you turned there were Smith girls. Jesus, what a family, and Ed had one child before he drank himself to death. That turned out to be Cousin Charles, who's following in his father's footsteps; you've seen him.

"And that's all that's left of the goddamn family. The only one, outside of old Cotton, who carries the family name is Cousin Charles and he ain't about to beget any little Savages, so the name is going to die, except on a map."

Sally said, "You should listen to yourself. Sour grapes."

He looked at her in surprise. "I don't envy a one of them. In fact, while I have to admit I have no use for Cousin Charles, I actually admire the old robber baron and I sort of like Queen Alice and I'm practically in love with Virginia Goldsboro because at least she has character. She honestly believes in this environmental protection crap, but she fights like a man. In her battle against the boatyard, she wasn't trying to knife me in the back, she was coming straight at me trying to cut off my balls."

"So you're in love with her," Sally scoffed.

"Not really. Hey, I'll tell you who's in love with her. Her Cousin Charles. He follows her around like a drunken puppy. He was steered into a marriage a long time ago to some mousy little girl, but it didn't last long. He comes on as a harmless, good-natured lush, doesn't he? Don't you believe it. He once got it in his fool head that I was going to attack Virginia. I did have a hammer in my hand and maybe I would have tapped her lightly on the skull, I don't know, I was that mad, but this lovable tub of lard grabbed me and broke my thumb. I thought he was going to kill me and I'm no weakling. I sent them the doctor's bill and they paid it. That damn thumb still gives me trouble.

"Now take Virginia, she doesn't need him to do her strong-arm work. She could do it herself if she had a mind to, but I think she likes having Cousin Charles around. Maybe that's how she gets her jollies.

"I don't want to give you the wrong impression

of Virginia. I don't think she's a dyke, not a prac-
ticing one, anyway. I'll tell you what she is, she's a
tomboy who never grew out of it. When she was a
kid, her Uncle Cotton liked playing with her. He
took her sailing a lot. But as she got tweedier and
tweedier, he got turned off. He's really a lonely
old bastard. The only one he really likes is his
sister; he can't stand the others.

"I told you I liked Virginia. I do. I think when
God the Uncle turned away from her, she was hurt
badly. It's my theory that she figured the old man
wanted a boy, so she tried to be more and more
like a boy. And you can see where that got her. So
much for my jiffy psychoanalysis. The fact is she
likes to be in the company of men, slap them on
the back. And they like her well enough, only they
laugh at her, too.

"Who am I to feel sorry for her? She has more
energy than Con Edison. I knew a crappy writer
who wanted to write fancy so he wrote about
someone having joie de vivre. That's what Virginia
has, joie de vivre. She's into everything and enjoying the hell out of it. She's not only the mad pro-
tector of the wetlands; she's a bird-watcher
extraordinary, a leader of the Girl Scouts, a demon
duck hunter, a powerful swimmer, a lover of sailing though she never goes near the *Lord Jim*, I
don't know why, and a part-time real-estate
agent, as you well know. She does that strictly for
the money. Old Cotton isn't very good at handing
out pocket money. She would have been president
of the civic association, except that there's never
been a woman president. Well, never mind, she's
active in everything. She even plays the organ at

church. You've heard her. Have you ever heard anything so god-awful? No one has the nerve to tell her, so she keeps playing."

Sally broke in. "Where does Steve fit into all this?"

"Nowhere. You asked about the Savages, so I'm telling you. Have you heard enough?"

"Oh, please, yes." She added quickly, "No. I mean I want to find out anything at all that could have the remotest bearing on Steve's death. Would any of them have any reason to want to kill him? If not, I'm back where I started. Nowhere." Suddenly she had to get out of the chair. She jumped up and started to straighten the pile of clothes on the bed.

"Don't move around. You can be seen from outside." He blocked the window with his body while · she crept back to her chair. He patted her hand. "I'm sorry, honey, I don't know of any connection. Only that his parents lived here for a short while more than thirty years ago, but I don't know if they ever even met the Savages—though they were neighbors—much less got involved with them. The only other possible connection is Steve's law firm. Did he work on any case for them?"

. "No," she said. "Walter Keller handles their affairs."

"Then maybe it's something that's come up since you moved here. You'd know better than me about that. You've met them all, haven't you?"

"All except the old man. Funny thing, we were going to be introduced to him today if he felt up to it. I got the impression there's something wrong with him. Is he seriously ill?"

"If you call being eighty-one serious, yes. And if you call having a stroke that's put him in a wheel-chair serious, yes, he ain't doing too good. That happened about ten years ago. There was gossip at the time that the family wanted to have him declared incompetent so they could get their hands on his dough, but I don't know if there was any truth to it. In any case, he's still in the driver's seat, and he's too ornery to die just to please them."

The hand was on hers, big, callused, strong yet gentle, comforting her. She didn't want him to take it away. Her mind slowed down to a blessed blankness and her eyes started to close. Genuine concern showed in his eyes, but his mouth said, "You're tough on husbands, aren't you?" Her eyes popped open, and he said quickly, "I mean you've had tough luck with husbands."

"Are you going to call the police?"

He took his hand away and turned from her. "No, I'm waiting for them to post a reward." He looked at her with hurt eyes. "Do you really think I would turn you in?"

"You're the first one to mention Willie Spencer, as if I killed both Willie and Steve."

"I didn't mention him, but I'll tell you who did. The newscaster on the radio. They're calling you 'Little Sally' all over again. Little Sally, who went on trial for the death of her first husband, the Olympic runner Willie Spencer, is now a fugitive from the police in connection with the shotgun slaying of her second husband, attorney Stephen Cochran, in their one hundred and fifty thousand dollar home on affluent Savage Point."

"One hundred and fifty thousand dollars!"

"Journalistic inflation, honey. Hey, I didn't mean to knock off old scabs, I was just trying to be sympathetic, for Christ's sake. And I was about to say you look bushed. Why don't you lie down for a while?" He took the pile of clothes from the bed and dumped them on the leather chair. Mumbling thanks, she let him lead her to the bed, feeling safe in the encircling arm. Her bag of possessions was looped to her wrist by the drawstrings. "If you hear two loud raps on the door, hop into the trunk, y'hear?" She dozed, thrusting aside the thought that she was being a traitor to Steve. At least she was free to keep looking for his murderer, which she wouldn't be able to do from a cuckoo's nest.

Her fitful sleep was disturbed several times, once when some boys came to visit Barney, once when a boat owner delivered his boat for winter storage, another time by a woman's voice. She dreamed of the nurse at Kings County who kept saying to her, "You're an Olympic star, Sally Spencer, the whole country loves you." She did more for her than the whole squad of psychiatrists. Sally felt warmed. . . .

The two raps. For a moment she stood quivering in the middle of the room, holding the mesh bag, groping for reality. Through the front window, she saw the police car rolling across the dirt patch toward her. She backed away from the open trunk, looked frantically around for an alternative. She hadn't noticed the small back window before. Out front, the police car was coming to a halt. She groaned; the back window looked too

small for her to get through, the police would find
her caught, frozen, half in and half out.. . .

She kicked out the screen, heard it land in the
water, went feet first through the window, wrig-
gled her hips; they were caught, then they were
through, and she was hanging from the window
ledge over the channel. She pulled the bag
through, then, chinning herself on the sill, she
reached and pulled the window down to where it
was open about two inches. It would have to do.
She gazed down into the muddy water and
dropped, body rigid, toes pointed. Her feet went
into muck, her head under water. In revulsion,
she sprang straight up, partially out of the water,
realizing she could now be seen from the big window in Barney's office. She clung to the slimy rock
wall that was the foundation of Barney's building,
edged along it, out of sight from the police unless
they opened the window and looked down. Had
they heard the noise of the screen, the splash, her
gasping? They must have, she thought, pulling
away in frenzy as she heard Barney's rasping
voice, intentionally loud, saying, "Gentlemen, I
am thrice honored. What's this sudden interest in
boating? You know what they say, sailors have
more fun." He had obviously seen her T-shirt, and
the slogan babbled out of him for want of something to say.

The channel ended where the tree line dipped
down to the marsh. She clambered on hands and
knees into the tall reeds, snapping some, for long
seconds open to view from the boathouse. Fifty
feet in, she stopped. The palm of her left hand was
bleeding, and she was whimpering again. She held

her breath and listened, but there was no sound of pursuit. She was soaked and filthy. She checked the bag; some water had seeped into the top layer, the sweater was wet, but the dress at the bottom was dry. She was still too close to the police. She had to move on, back toward Savage Point, with no place to go. She felt degraded; her panting sounded like that of a wild animal. The wet clothing stuck to her uncomfortably. A sense of defeat crushed her. She rose to a half-crouch, intending to go back and give herself up. The thought of Barney made her stop. Her emergence out of his swamp could bring him trouble. She would make her way to the other side of Savage Point, far from Barney's place, and let herself be captured there. She crept through the revolting swamp, whimpering.

Willie Spencer would have laughed and called her a sad sack, short for a sad sack of shit. He'd have told her to go the chaplain and get a "T.S. slip," an Army joke implying that all a chaplain could do would be to cluck sympathetically and say, "Tough shit." Willie had had a rough mouth, like Barney's, which he had acquired in Vietnam. He had literally run away from that corner of hell by excelling as a middle-distance runner. When the brass had discovered he could beat every other American at the 440, they brought him back to the States and entered him in the '72 Olympics under the U.S. Army's own colors. He had won a bronze medal for them at Munich in that ill-fated meet. The world was full of sad sacks. Tough, fellas.

But why not go to the chaplain, for Pete's sake? What's more natural than a troubled member of the flock seeking guidance and consolation from the good shepherd? Pastor John might even be of some help. Perhaps convince the police she wasn't the insane killer they thought she was. Besides, what did she have to lose? If he sternly turned his back on her and called the police, let him have the credit, what the hell. She was going to turn herself in, anyway. Same difference.

She sat on a shelf of rock beneath Harper Road and cleaned her face and hands, combed her hair as best she could. The jeans and T-shirt were starting to dry, fitting her form more snugly than before. She stood up and began walking.

At Savage Road, she found she had come a block too far. This was the corner with the burned-out house, standing there as a creepy warning that people who live in wooden houses shouldn't sleep like stones. It had happened shortly after she and Steve had moved to the point, and Pastor John had emerged as a hero, raising a ladder to the second floor to rescue two children and a dog. The block was a short one, with only the two houses on it, the minister's and this one. The rest of the block, marked off by high hedges, was taken up by Greystone and the great lawn sloping to the Shore Road and the seawall.

She went behind the charred hulk, quickly rolled the jeans above her knees, took off the Cardozo jacket, pulled on the blue dress over the T-shirt and jeans. The dress was badly wrinkled, but the blue sweater mercifully covered much of it. The pink scarf over her head hid the fact that her hair was cut. She changed the sneakers for the high-heeled shoes. She was disguising her disguise from Pastor John. She just wasn't ready to give anything from her pitiful store of options.

4:30. ONE OF THE BLOND CHILDREN opened the door, backed away into his mother's skirt. Emma Dantine had the attractively plump look of German health, round face, red cheeks, blond hair. Wiping her hands on a kitchen towel, she gazed nearsightedly at Sally. "Oh," she said, backing through the inner door with the child. Sally understood her confusion; the minister's wife wasn't sure whether this was a parishioner in need or a handmaiden of the devil. "Mrs. Cochran." She backed into the living room, then left to get her husband. So far, a fiasco.

John Dantine was tall, rangy, quite handsome in a movie star sort of way; his wavy graying hair was too long to look neat and not long enough to be considered a mane. He spoke in the mellifluous tones of a second-rate Shakespearean actor. Sally was betting her life that beneath the dramatic image was a real person.

He led her to his study, where he had a desk, two comfortable chairs and a large bookcase. He invited Sally to sit in one of the chairs. He sat behind the desk, and said, "Shall we start with a prayer?"

"No, please. I mean I don't have much time," she said nervously.

He looked at her with his piercing gaze, which he had practiced for just such moments as this. "You are safe here," he intoned. "This is a sanctuary for contrite sinners, no matter what they have done. Are you contrite, Sally Cochran?"

Quashing an impulse to laugh that she knew would slide into hysterical crying, she said, "I'm sorry for everything that's happened, but I didn't kill my husband, if that's what you mean. It's not my sin, Pastor John."

"Then why are you running from the police?"

"Because," she said. She had difficulty saying the words. "Because they've already convicted me in their minds. They'll put me in an asylum for the rest of my life. I couldn't stand that."

He came around the desk, sat on the arm of the chair next to hers, put his hand on her shoulder. The moves and the excessive sincerity in the voice were practiced. "I believe you, Sally Cochran," he said. "But you are wrong to run from them. It is not theirs to decide whether you go into a mental institution or not. That would be up to a court and jury. Nobody has convicted you. Except yourself, by running away. Give yourself up, Mrs. Cochran, and trust in God to bring out the truth."

"That's exactly what I can't do, Pastor John," she said, surprised at the sound of a decision made. "Don't you see, somebody in Savage Point murdered my husband and made it look like I did it, knowing that with my history everybody would be willing to believe it. Including you, Pastor John."

His hand fell from her shoulder. "I'm trying to believe you, Sally," he said softly. "Give me a chance to believe you." The real person was emerging, she thought with a flicker of hope.

In a flat voice, she told him her meager recollections of the murder.

He said, "The police are all over the place. How have you been able to stay out of their sight?"

She smiled and told him about the duck blind, immediately regretting it, for she didn't know what righteous impulses flashed through the man that might cause him to turn on her. She had come to get information, not give it. She asked about the Savage family.

"Good people," he replied. "I warn you I am not an unbiased observer. You can't know the extent of their blessed support for the church. I wouldn't be here if it weren't for that generous family. I pray for them every day in my prayers."

"I'm trying to believe you, Pastor John," she said ironically, adding quickly, "I do believe you. I have no reason to doubt that they are anything but devout Christian people. But there has to be a motive for Steve's murder, I don't know what it is, but it involves the Savage family, I'm convinced of that. Otherwise I'd have to agree with the police—it was done by a crazy person."

The minister slid down into the chair. "What do you want to know?"

"Anything that might be some sort of a link between Steve and the Savage family. Even if it doesn't seem like a link." John Dantine was shaking his head slowly. "Steve's law firm handled the family's business. Do you know anything about that?"

"I am only consulted on spiritual matters," he said. "I have a poor head for finance. Walter Keller would know more about that."

"Did you know that his parents once lived in this house? That's another connection."

"Whose parents? This house? You must be mistaken. This has been the minister's house for decades."

"Exactly. James Cotton Savage bought it from Steve's father and gave it to the church. That was about thirty years ago."

He said, "What does that prove? Is there a motive for murder in an ancient act of charity?"

"No," she said. "I was hoping you knew something more."

He said, "The deed's in the safe-deposit box, but I don't think it would tell us anything."

She sighed. "Neither do I. But there's one person who can tell something about it, and that's James Cotton Savage himself. I'm going to talk to him first chance I get."

Suddenly the pastor wasn't friendly anymore. He stood, towering above her. "You will not talk to him. You will not bother him. I won't stand for it. Do you hear me, Mrs. Cochran? As for your husband, I can assure you that James Cotton Savage did not shoot him. He couldn't, he's crippled, he can't move anywhere without the wheelchair. He couldn't hold a shotgun, his left arm is withered. As for hearing what he might have to say, I doubt if you'd understand him. His speech is affected. A visit from you can only disturb him and can't help you. I want you to agree not to go near him."

She looked up at him, feeling bruised and defiant. "I can't promise that."

John Dantine moved around the desk and sat down. "I'll make a bargain. If you promise not to bother him, I'll promise not to call the police."

She gasped. "I thought you said this was a sanctuary. Isn't the pastor-parishioner relationship privileged? I thought you were bound not to tell. How could you?"

He leaned back in the chair. "It's a gray area,"

he said. "I don't believe I would reveal what you said to me here, but I don't think the mere fact of your presence is covered. Do you promise?"

"I promise not to bother him," she said meekly, mentally reserving the right to interpret the word *bother* in her own way.

"Good," he said, relaxing his stern posture. "Now I'll tell you who you ought to talk to. Virginia Goldsboro. She should know of anything involving your husband. Or talk to Dr. Everett Smith. He's been the family physician for thirty-five years. He treated Mr. Savage when he had the stroke ten years ago. I'm told he treated Cotton's wife in her terminal illness thirty years ago, he goes that far back. He and Walter Keller were called in when the question of Cotton's competency was raised—" He abruptly stopped speaking, as if he had said more than was discreet. "All of that was before I came here. So you see, you ought to talk to one of them, not me. Not I," he corrected himself incorrectly.

Reverting to sanctimony, he said he was forgetting his pastoral duties and asked if there was anything he could do. Perhaps regarding the funeral. She asked him to get together with Walter Keller and arrange what needed to be done. She told him where Steve's mother could be reached. Thinking of her for the first time, she was suddenly sure that Bess Cochran would not come to Savage Point but would probably have Steve brought to Mamaroneck.

And she added Bess Cochran to the list of people she should talk to, for she had lived in this very house and would surely know if there had been any contact between the two families. Besides the

deed, that is. But Bess would have to wait. Getting
from Savage Point to Westchester would be a per-
ilous journey, her reception of Sally might be
hostile, and the police would probably have
staked out her home.

Pastor John graciously asked her if she'd like to
see the house that was once occupied by her
parent-in-law. To Sally, houses weren't interesting, only furnishings, but she said she'd be delighted. Emma was outside the study, wiping her hands
on the dish towel. Apparently a major occupation
with her, Sally thought. The house was neat,
clean, sparsely furnished with inexpensive ob-
jects, uninteresting. On the second floor the slightly larger bedroom, thus the master bedroom, faced
west. Higher than the giant privet hedge, the window overlooked the rear facades of Greystone,
whose unlovely bulk blocked the view of Little
Neck Bay and the green shores of Bayside. Even if
Steve's parents had had no social contacts with
the holy family, Sally decided, they did have a fine
peeping-Tom view of Greystone's rear windows.
Maybe they saw something they shouldn't have
seen that made them a menace to the family's
well-being. Maybe Mike and Bess tried to black-
mail Cotton Savage and were railroaded out of
town for their efforts. Maybe Mike tried to seduce
the virginal Edith or the teenage Virginia and
reaped the laird's eternal enmity unto the seventh
generation. Maybe. . . .

6:05. SWINGING ALONG KING'S ROAD, she was the
consummate high-school junior, aware that the
tight jeans flaunted her rear end at every step,

feeling more naked than she ever had in leotards. Her faith in her disguise made her careless.

"Hey, kid," the man's voice said, "come here." The blue Volvo had stopped at the side of the road, and Boomer Smith leaned across the front seat toward her. He didn't look as though he were there to compliment her.

Sally looked around. There was no one else on the sidewalk. "Me?" she asked.

"Yes, you, you dummy. Come here." The voice was a command.

She got in. Breathing heavily, she stared fixedly ahead, humiliated in every way but especially by the fact that it was this detestable man who had caught her.

He smiled at her in an apparent attempt to reassure her. "Okay?" he asked.

She nodded.

He started to drive slowly, without goal, neglecting to avoid the many potholes that were badges of Savage Points' self-induced isolation. "You're bad news, Mrs. Cochran," he said, keeping his voice to a low rumble. "I'm sorry to say that because I was looking forward to playing doctor with you. Those Seconals I gave your husband, they were for you, weren't they?"

She shrugged.

"I thought so." He turned left on Dover, passing a police car. "You're a disaster for Savage Point. We're all over the television news, and we don't like it. That sort of publicity is hurting us. We're infested with police cars like we were some kind of Harlem."

"I didn't do it," she said in a small voice.

"Hell, Sally, I don't care whether you did it or not," he boomed. "That's not what I'm talking about. But your running from the police and your persistent disregard for the feelings of your neighbors, that's unforgivable. There's a TV crew right there," he said, pointing angrily. "Don't you see what you've caused?" He turned onto Harper Road. Some cars were parked alongside the cove. "Sightseers! We're overrun with sightseers! And they're all illegally parked! That's the sort we want to keep out of here! Law violators! Look, they're throwing their litter all over the place!"

She said, "Doesn't it make any difference that I'm innocent?"

"Hey, you can't park there!" he called to one of the cars. The people looked at him as though he were the intruder. "We'll see!" he called, and sped up, mumbling, "Where are the cops when you need them?" He turned to her. "They looked like they were Puerto Rican, didn't they?" he asked in an outraged voice.

"Dr. Smith, I want you to tell me a few things."

"Anything, anything, only it's Boomer. Even now I think of you as a friend. It's just that—"

She interrupted. "Will you answer some questions for me?"

"Will you give yourself up?"

"Yes, after you've answered my questions." She didn't say how long after. She was getting adept at making mental reservations.

He drove to a quiet road that made a loop by the railroad cut, inappropriately called Piccadilly, where there were no houses. He cut off the motor and said, "Shoot."

"First, why were you out looking for me?"

"Walter Keller and I talked it over. We thought it best."

"He's out trying to track me down, too?"

"That was the idea."

"It's nice to feel wanted," she said. "Okay, what's the connection between Steve and the Savage family?"

"I don't know of any, except Virginia Goldsboro was your broker. You're new in the neighborhood, remember."

"His parents lived here thirty years ago."

"Is that a fact?"

"What went on between them and the Savages?"

"Nothing." He started humming, tapping his fingers on the wheel.

"They were next-door neighbors."

"That doesn't mean anything. Take my own neighbors, I say hello to them, that's all."

"You're not answering my questions."

"You're not asking many."

"Something happened here about thirty years ago. The Cochrans moved out of the area, Cotton Savage's wife died, and the rest of the Savages moved into Greystone, where they've lived happily ever after. What happened?"

He was looking at her with a little more interest. "You're obviously cooking up a story in your mind. What makes you think I would know anything about this story of yours?"

"You were the family doctor."

"I had barely hung out my shingle."

"You were a relative. Isn't Cousin Charles your cousin, too?"

"Don't hold that against me."

"What did Cotton's wife die of?"

"I'd have to look that up."

"I was told you attended her in her last illness."

"That was a long time ago."

"Did she die of natural causes?"

"What do you mean by that?"

"I mean, was she in an accident? She was a fairly young woman, wasn't she?"

"Fifty."

"You do remember it well, don't you?"

He sighed. "She did not die as a result of an accident."

"Was she, by any chance, murdered?"

"In Savage Point? That sort of thing simply doesn't happen here."

"It did. Last night. This morning. I'm wondering if there was a precedent. A previous shotgun murder."

"Edith Savage was not murdered," he shouted angrily. "By shotgun or otherwise. She died of a perfectly ordinary, everyday heart attack. It was in May. She was aboard the *Lord Jim*. I'd told her not to do anything strenuous, but she loved the boat. The launch service doesn't start until June, so she had rowed out. When I got the call, I had to be rowed out, too. By Cousin Charles. She was dead. End of story. Now, it's your turn to live up to—"

"I'm not finished. Was that before or after the Cochrans moved out?"

"I don't remember. I don't think the two events are related." He looked away from her, but she could feel a tenseness in him that wasn't there before.

She was sure the two events *were* related and she had to keep the questions coming. "When Cotton had his stroke ten years ago, who tried to have him declared incompetent?"

He thumped the wheel impatiently. "Come off it, Mrs. Cochran, that can have no bearing whatsoever on your husband's death."

"You were the family physician. They wouldn't have tried to have him declared mentally incompetent without your say-so."

"Look, they were sincerely worried about him. Walter Keller, too. I told all of them that Cotton's speech may have been affected but not his mind. That it was sharp as ever, give or take a few hardening arteries. They were reassured and dropped the whole matter. Who's been spreading that old gossip?"

"Old gossip is all I have to go on." She looked at him with pleading eyes. "Maybe it's just an insane story I've made up, as you say, but there's one man who can say whether it is or not. Boomer, please, I have to talk to Cotton Savage. Will you help me? Just take me to see Cotton, and then you can call the police."

"Not on your life," he said, turning the key in the ignition. "Not on your life." Coldly, he said, "I think I've answered all your questions. Now, are you going to the police?"

She shook her head numbly. "Not yet. I can't."

"Wait, I have an idea," he said brightly. "You like Walter Keller, don't you? You trust him, don't you?"

She nodded in the same numb fashion.

"Fine, then why don't we just ride over to his house, and you and he can talk about it."

"No," she cried. "It's right next door. The police'll be there."

"That's good," he said, even more brightly. "Then you can give yourself up."

She shook her head rather like a stunned animal, slowly in a low arc. He had put his hand lightly on hers. In a quick move, he gripped her wrist and, with the other hand, snatched up a hypodermic syringe from beneath a cloth on the dashboard.

"I thought you might get stubborn," he muttered as he sought to plunge the needle into her arm "so—I—" Because he was holding her in an awkward way and because he little expected such strength from a woman, she was able to swivel her arm and pull loose, causing the needle to go into the ball of his hand. She wrenched the door open and slithered out as he made a sideways lunge at her, missing.

Knowing she couldn't outrun a car, she headed for the Goat Trail, a dirt path that ran somewhat perilously, and quite illegally, along the edge of the railroad track all the way to the Savage Point station. The trail ended on the east side of Savage Road; the station was at the foot of a flight of stairs.

She crouched and started the painful passage beneath the north platform, trying to run in the crouched position, part duck walk, part Russian kick dance, cracking her head at one moment, scraping her knees in the gravel the next, praying that no one would blunder onto the opposite platform from which she was in full view. Just as it seemed that the platform was interminable and that she would never come to the end, she was there, sobbing quietly. On hands and knees, she inched her head forward to see around the edge.

Here the track bed sloped down to the marsh, out of sight from the station. She looked over the tops of the reeds at the ill-conceived colony of houses that had been built on the marsh bordering Dover Road and the more expensive homes on the old Cotton property. She could see the innocent blue of the police car trying to be inconspicuous at the western end. Obviously, Savage Point was being honored by a cordon blue, and she was the prize. She darted down the slope and into the reeds, back in the swamp from which she couldn't seem to escape.

And again she had no place to go. Without actually planning, she had assumed she could go back to the duck blind for shelter in the night. Now it seemed that someone had informed the police about her temporary refuge, for they were patently making a more determined effort to keep her penned in on the point. She tried to remember who knew about it. Joey Dee. Barney Harper. Pastor John. The information was probably community property by now. Even so, she decided to make her way around the homes on the Cotton property, which jutted into Little Neck Bay, and check out the surveillance at the blind.

"Mrs. Cochran." The hoarse whisper came from somewhere above her. She looked up in the deepening dusk, and saw Joey Dee sitting on the seawall. He beckoned her to the stone steps. At the top, he led her behind a yew.

"I was waiting for you," he said with tears in his voice. "There wasn't anything I could do. Just wait and hope you'd come by this way and not from over there." He pointed beyond the distant duck blind to the other edge of the swamp. "They're waiting for you."

She nodded. "I kinda thought so." She started to sob, which set Joey to sobbing.

"Okay," he said fiercely, "that's enough. Come on in."

"Your father," she said.

"It's all right. Come on."

The DiGiorgio home was a strange mixture of cold chrome and hot Florentine colors. She thought of the hues as Florentine, but they were probably Sicilian. The blue bottles and vases in the window were definitely from Florence; the illuminated Sacred Heart in the corner was probably Sicilian. Johnny Dee, a powerful man of average height, welcomed her with a smile and a shoulder hug; his wife, Gemma, a short round woman, asked solicitously, "Have you eaten?"

"I'm filthy," Sally said, fearing to step on the deep-pile red rug.

Sensation returned to her in the shower. The warm water was pleasantly sensual and a catalyst of profound sadness, reminding her that captivity would bring animal comfort while freedom promised only continued pain. The stings of her cuts broke the mood, and she found she was hungry.

Gemma said *mangia* five times during the conversation in the kitchen. She spoke with an Italian accent, Johnny Dee with a Brooklyn accent, Joey with a north Queens and Sally with faint overtones of her native Alabama, while she worked on a leftover portion of sirloin, broccoli and spaghetti. Two younger children were half hidden by the refrigerator, watching.

When Sally had once again described the meager details of Steve's murder, Johnny Dee growled, "Sounds almost like a hit. Something a professional might do."

"You mean a hired killer?" she asked in surprise. She had assumed that the person who wanted Steve dead was the one who pulled the trigger.

DiGiorgio looked embarrassed. "I only meant that if someone put out a contract on Steve, that's the way the hit man would blast him away. Only one thing wrong. He wouldn't use Steve's gun. He'd use his own, one that he knew and trusted. Maybe we shouldn't talk like this about your husband."

"Is it usual—" Sally tried to phrase her question diplomatically. "Is it usual for a private person, I mean one who's not a member of the—do you call them families—to put out a contract and have a professional hit man do the job?"

"It'd have to be done through a member," he said tersely. "And it probably wouldn't be okayed. Okay?"

"Please, I wasn't implying anything, just trying to get information. I believe someone on Savage Point killed Steve. But you raise the possibility that the killer hired someone to do it rather than do it himself."

"S'okay, Mrs. Cochran. But if one of these snooty Anglo-Saxon—" With difficulty he held back the blistering expletive he was about to utter, lamely substituted "persons." "If one of them hired a killer, it woulda been an amateur, not a pro."

"Do you belong to a family?" she asked.

His smile seemed to say he was amused. "Mafia? Naah. I know some of the paisanos, they done favors for me, I done favors for them, but I don't belong to no one. Sometimes we play ball and then I go home, y'know what I mean? It's the Sicilian version of the old school tie. We're looked on as outsiders, so we form an outsiders' league, see."

"You're talking about Savage Point?"

"Don't get me started on that, Mrs. Cochran. I could buy and sell half of these superior, er, people, so it ain't the money. I guess it's what they call culture. Take opera. They like to talk about the opera, but the Joe from Italy who's cutting their hair knows more about opera than they do, only he can't talk about it very good."

Sally said, "You were angry at my husband."

"I was? No, I wasn't mad at your husband."

"You thought he was mishandling your case."

"Do you call that mad? Sure, I had a discussion with him maybe a couple of times. Serious discussions. I'll tell you what about. It was about the district attorney wants to put me in jail, take me away from my wife and family, take away my house, the food on the table. That's serious. But mad, I wasn't mad at Stevie boy. I think he's a hell of a lawyer. He got *you* off, didn't he?"

"Was that a hard thing to do?"

"Now don't you start getting mad at me! You're a member of the outsiders' league, remember? Welcome to the club."

Joey heard something, and slipped outside to investigate. Gemma said to the two younger kids, "Don't touch that shade. Stay away from the win-

dow." DiGiorgio said, "We may have to stash
you," waiting for Joey's report.

"Were the police here today?" Sally asked.

"Twice. Just to gab and say if Mrs. Cochran
shows up here, blah, blah, and we say sure sure,
sure we will. But they didn't try to search the
house. If they come around with a search warrant,
that's a different story."

Joey came back to say that a police car was
parked outside the house and he could hear their
radio going, but it looked like they were just coop-
ing.

Sally said, "Are you guilty of extortion, Mr.
DiGiorgio?"

"You like to ask snotty questions, don't you?"
He stopped her reply by saying, "I know, you're
only looking for information." He sighed. "It's a
rough world, Mrs. Cochran. I have a nice, legitimate business going. It's not exactly classy, picking up garbage, but it's an honorable business.
Some other bonehead tries to muscle in, and I muscle back. If he scares a customer, I lean on the
customer a little harder. Just trying to keep my
business going."

Returning to the living room, they were discuss-
ing where she could safely pass the night, when
the ring of the doorbell held them rigid for the second it took the youngest child to open the door.
The policeman came in, DiGiorgio cried, "Oh,
come in, officer," Sally plopped into a stuffed
chair and, swinging a leg over the arm, looked at
the policeman insolently, and the policeman said,
"Just checking, Mr. DiGiorgio. Have you heard
from her?"

Johnny Dee affably patted the cop on the back, complimented him on his diligence, steered him out the door. His face was tight when he turned back. "They're not looking for a teenager yet, but they will," he said. "Joey, take your young girlfriend out to the boat, and make sure you button it down right. Mrs. Cochran, you make a good-looking teenager, but you're a danger to Johnny Dee, who don't need no more trouble than he's got already. If they search the boat, you've had it. They done it once this afternoon, and I'm betting they won't do it again."

Sally offered to just go away and not cause them trouble, but DiGiorgio growled, "Don't talk nonsense. Go with Joey. Good night, Mrs. Cochran."

The Cotton property was a dead spot in the police cordon; the land abutting the bay was all private property, no road touched on the waterfront. The sky was as dark as it ever gets in New York City; the clouds had come on quickly, but the millions of reflected lights in the atmosphere dimly bathed the bay. Joey came out of the boat room with an inflated rubber dinghy, carried it down the seawall steps, eased it quietly into the water. They lay on their stomachs, a tight squeeze in the small craft, Joey leaning forward of the nose with a paddle. Slowly, noiselessly, he inched the craft out into the middle of the bay. Sally raised her head, saw with dismay the clear outline of the shore. Surely the watching eyes must see this lone, lumpy thing moving strangely across the gray water, an unidentified floating object. She lowered her head and waited.

She must have dozed, for she was startled when

Joey touched her shoulder. He was clinging to the side of a cabin cruiser. Grimacing with the effort to muffle the snapping sound, he partially unbuttoned the protective canvas. He held open the flap, silently indicated for her to crawl in. He followed. She stood still in the darkness, while he found a flashlight, covered it with his sweater and flicked it on. In the dim light he showed her to the cabin, touched the bunk and the blankets in a chest, opened the door to the cramped head. Still in pantomime, he showed her the thin curtains over the windows, the larder, small refrigerator, butane gas burner. He looked at her questioningly, she gave him an okay sign. She pointed to him and whispered, "When?" He put a finger to his lips, and mouthed, "One-thirty. After school."

He gave her a towel with which to smother the light, flipped it off and placed it in her hands. Then he was gone. The darkness closed in on her.

ALONE IN A CELL. Little Sally has done it again, folks, said the announcer in her head. For the third time. Wait, you're only counting her two husbands. You didn't know that she killed her parents, too. She was too small to lift an ax, of course, since she was only three. But she killed them. She was on the floor in the backseat of the car, playing with something, she doesn't remember what. When the smashup came, she wasn't even bruised, though it did put an end to the game. She remembers crying because she couldn't continue the game and she couldn't get out of the backseat. She didn't cry for her mother and father. When the highway patrolman lifted her out, she cried again because she didn't want to leave her parents, not because they were dead. Later, she knew something was wrong with the fact that she had survived and they hadn't. It made her feel guilty. She still feels guilty, folks, and rightly so, because she had been mad at them and then they died. Therefore, Little Sally had caused their death. She also saw the link between where she lived, Mobile, and the automobile that killed them. She didn't like Mobile.

Her Uncle Joe and Aunt Tina took her in and tried to become her parents. They're gone now, but they must have been pretty nice people. They encouraged her gymnastics in high school, and even sent her for a year to the University of Alabama, though they really couldn't afford it and there weren't any scholarships for gymnastics. She was a freshman, eighteen going on nineteen, when she went to Munich as America's darling Little Sally to compete against Russia's darling little Olga Korbut. Little Sally looked very good, you must remember her, she won our hearts if not the Olympic gold medal. A lot of Americans thought she was cheated out of the top prize by prejudiced judges.

And now, what about Willie Spencer, the announcer in her head droned on. He was a street kid from St. Louis, four years older and infinitely more experienced. Vietnam aged children quickly. To the timid little gymnast, Willie Spencer was glamorous, funny, exciting, unpredictable—he did wild things on the spur of the moment—and irresistibly masculine. They literally panted for each other, I'm told, but could do nothing about it in

the segregated Olympic Village; then the slaughter
of the Israeli athletes put a damper on everything,
including sex. But the night after the close of the
games they broke training. Several times, as a matter of fact.

This unusual pair of lovers—the orphan from
Mobile and the urchin from St. Louis—returned to
the United States and got married. But they didn't
live happily ever after. No, sirree, it was more like
a year. The wedding made national news; the
whole country was happy for them. But the end of
the marriage made *international* news!

The scene is the roof of a twelve-story apart-
ment building in Brooklyn Heights. It's a warm
summer evening— How did they wind up in
Brooklyn Heights? That's easily explained.
Neither of them wanted to go back to their home-
towns. Jobs were easy for an Olympic medalist to
get, even a bronze medalist, so Willie accepted a
job on Wall Street and he joined the New York
Athletic Club to continue his running. Brooklyn
Heights is a five-minute subway trip from Wall
Street. It's an area with a spectacular view of
Manhattan and the harbor, from the Statue of
Liberty to the Brooklyn Bridge. So that's where
these lovebirds set up their nest.

As I say, it was a warm summer evening, and
some of the apartment dwellers were on the roof,
catching the cool breeze off the bay, mooning over
the vista, having cocktails, chatting lazily. What
was Little Sally doing? Cutting string beans! Isn't
that what you said you were doing, Sally? Right!
Cutting string beans, and what was Willie Spencer
doing? Horsing around at the edge of the roof! He

was happy. They were celebrating some good
news, what was it, a raise? He had just been given
a raise by his Wall Street firm.

We have here an eyewitness to the bizarre event
that occurred on that roof that evening. Mrs. Shir-
ley Hazeltine lives in the same Grace Court apartment building. She and her husband Harold were
up on the roof to get some air. Tell us what you
told the court at the trial, Mrs. Hazeltine.

"Well, as I told the jury, my husband Harold and
I often go up to the roof for an hour or so, it's so
pleasant and relaxed. We take our camp chairs and
we have iced tea. I remember it was our first iced
tea of the summer. There were four or five other
groups up there, and we knew them all and we
chewed the fat and all that. The Spencers were off
to themselves, near the back corner, that would
be the southwest corner, I think, I get mixed up on
things like that. And he was sort of jumping
around like he couldn't keep still. You know, he
always frightened me a little bit because you
never knew what he was going to do next. Not
that he wasn't nice, he was very nice but erratic,
if you know what I mean.

"Well, we were just sitting there gabbing with
the Brunos, but I was facing the Spencers. Little
Sally was sitting there with a colander in her lap—I
always thought of her as a dear little thing, like a
Barbie doll—and her young man was showing off.
Really, it was a foolish thing for him to do, walk
like a little boy imitating a tightrope walker on the
wall at the edge of the roof, but I knew he was an
athlete, so I didn't worry. Well, there he was waving his arms and making whooping sounds, and all

of a sudden this Little Sally screamed, "Willie!"
She jumped from her chair, ran toward him with
the knife in her hand, she stabbed him here, sort
of the left side of the stomach, and he went over
backward. Oh, it was awful, I just sat there
speechless, wondering if I had seen what I just
saw. Ask Harold, I just sat there with my mouth
open—"

What did Little Sally do?

"Well, it looked like her lunge at him nearly
took her off the roof, too. Most of her was over,
but one hand had a hold of the parapet, is that
what you call it, so she pulled herself back on the
roof. Then she just sat there with her back to the
parapet, doing nothing, maybe moaning a little.
Her husband was dead, of course. I mean, twelve
stories, not even an Olympic athlete can do that."

Thank you, Mrs. Hazeltine. Now you will hear
from Little Sally herself. She will tell you her version of the story. Which, I must add, is the version
believed by the jury when they acquitted her. Listen to her story, folks, and then you be the judge.
Little Sally.

"I don't want to do this."

We know it's painful, Little Sally, but come on,
confession is good for the soul.

"This isn't a confession."

Of course, it isn't. It's just your version of the
story. Tell us, it'll make you feel better....

"Willie and I were very happy, you must believe
that. But we weren't very secure. People thought
we had the world by the tail, but we didn't. The
trouble was, Willie never went to college and here
he was in a job selling stocks and bonds, which

may sound easy, but it required a lot of knowledge he didn't have, and everybody he was working with was a college graduate. We were actually afraid he might get fired, so when they gave him a raise instead, wow, that was cause for a celebration.

"When he came home with the news, I already had a roast in the oven, so I said, 'Let's just have a little celebration tonight and save the big one for tomorrow.' I sent him out to get wine to go with the meal. Neither of us drank much, and having the wine would make it a special dinner. Well, he brought back gin and vermouth along with the wine, and he made martinis for us and suggested we drink them on the roof.

"That sounded like a good idea, but I hadn't done the string beans yet, so I brought them up with me and the knife I use to cut them, just a little kitchen knife. It was fun. Do you know what I felt like, sitting there cutting beans and talking and laughing with my husband—an old married woman! You may not believe it, it was the first time I had really felt that way, and it was pleasant.

"Willie didn't know how to drink. He gulped down the martini and wanted to start on mine, but I wouldn't let him. His spirits were already high, and the alcohol made him uncontrollable. We should have gone out to celebrate. I should have just turned off the oven and gone out with him, but I didn't.

"He did some handstands, he just couldn't sit still. Then he said, 'Watch this,' and started walking on the edge of the roof. I said, 'Willie, don't,' and then he started to lose his balance, waving his

arms out to the sides, teetering. I said, 'Willie!'
and jumped toward him to pull him away from the
edge. I tripped over the colander, which I had
knocked from my lap, I lost my balance and
couldn't stop myself. It was hard for people to
believe that a gymnast could be that clumsy. I find
it hard to believe, too, but it happened.

"I didn't realize I had the knife in my hand until
it cut him in the side. The coroner's report said it
was just a little scratch, and that's all it was. I was
trying to grab him, and couldn't. What I don't
know to this day is whether my stab wound
caused him to fall or whether he was falling backward even before the knife touched him. I have to
assume that the knife gave him the final push, and
that's my everlasting sorrow.

"I was looking down at him falling and I was
falling, too. I should have let go, but I didn't. If I
had let go, I would still be with him. I'm sorry for
that, too. I'm sorry about everything."

Two years have now gone by, folks. It's now the
time of the trial. Little Sally spent those years in a
mental institution. Let me put in a serious word
here. The fact that an alleged criminal spends two
years in a mental institution—or a loony bin or a
nut farm, I don't care what you call it—does not
mean that that criminal is guilty of the crime he or
she may or may not have committed before he or
she went to the crazy house. I want to stress
that—*does not*.

On the other hand, of course, when you listen to
her defense lawyer, Stephen Cochran, you have to
keep in mind that he's *on her side*, meaning he's
biased. Not that he'd lie to save his client's neck,

but when he says something, you may ask yourself, 'Do I have to believe him?' The answer is, you
do not, I repeat *do not*, have to believe him. Have I
stated that fairly, Mr. Cochran? Fine. It's your
turn, counsellor.

"Ladies and gentlemen, I want you to look
closely at Little Sally—don't turn your head away,
Sally—look at the little nose, the sad mouth, the
big eyes, the lovely figure. Does that look like the
face and figure of a liar? Golly, no, she's told you
the truth! She couldn't even lie about her parents' death. She told you the truth. She killed
them."

Sally squirmed in her sleep. This wasn't the way
it was, at all.

"Now, having forthrightly admitted a double
killing, would she lie to you about a measly single
killing? No! The fact is, she was in love with her
husband, and now she's in love with me, and I'm
in love with her, and we're going to be married.
And now, if you don't mind, I'm going to kiss her
and hold her until she's forgotten all the bad
things that have happened. And we're going to
live happily ever after."

ALONE IN A CELL. She had lain in his arms for a
long time, with her thumb in her mouth, and been
comforted. She had even giggled with him at her
feelings of guilt. Dawn, filtering through the light
curtains, had broken it up. Steve had returned to
being a bloody mess in their bed, the morning chill
had stolen beneath the blankets. Willie had receded to his place at the roof's edge, and Sally was
alone, in her cell, not much different from a prison

cell or one in an asylum, except that this one was
moving rhythmically and making her queazy.

6:05, Monday. She sat up. She was doomed to
stay here, on a gangster's boat, until half-past one,
unable to pursue a murderer who, disguised as a
solid citizen, had set up this quivering alumna of a
booby hatch for an unlimited postgraduate course,
and then had ratted on her to make sure that she
was securely signed on. A thought suddenly occurred to her. Was it possible that *she* was the
prime target of the killer and that the killing of
Steve was only the bloody means by which she
was to be put away? The thought made her doubt
her sanity.

2

7:20. SHE FOUND SOME DRAMAMINE in the larder, and took one. After a while, the dizziness and nausea disappeared. It was a cold, raw morning, the wind from the northeast bringing choppy water and a higher than normal tide in the bay. She had never been seasick before and this queasiness was a betrayal of her superbly healthy body, a first sign of decay. She sat on the bunk and shivered. The milk in the refrigerator was sour.

When she finally stirred, the decay had spread to her bones; her joints were stiff and she felt very old. She heated some of the bottled water on the burner and made coffee. Peanut butter and jelly, and some stale bread seemed to be the only food. It all tasted warming and delicious, and she soon knew for sure that she wasn't going to die.

She looked around the cabin in the glum daylight. It was small, but the open cockpit beyond the door, although enclosed in canvas, took the claustrophobic curse off it. To take her mind off the enforced inaction, she concentrated on knee bends, body twists, her whole regimen of limbering-up exercises. Her body felt good. She busied herself in tidying the bunk, folding the blankets, cleaning the breakfast things, making

another cup of coffee. She found the binoculars
beside the steering wheel.

Pushing up the curtain just enough, she focused
the lenses on Savage Point. "Wow," she said.
They were the most powerful binoculars she had
ever seen; each leaf of the trees on shore was
clearly defined. She couldn't see the duck blind
because of the reeds, but she could see a man in a
second-floor bedroom stepping into his trousers.
He had a sour look on his face. Slowly she swept
the shoreline from the point to the marsh and
around to the Cotton Estates where the DiGiorgios
lived. Despite snippets of human activity, which
flickered and vanished, there was a glowering
aspect to the scene, an ominous no-trespassing
feel to it, a tactile aura of hostility to outsiders, to
her. Even the yellow school buses seemed menacingly aloof.

She swung the glasses back to Greystone. It
reminded her of—she searched for the Greek
word—*hubris*, overweening arrogance in mortals
offensive to the gods. It squatted proudly on its
hillock, proclaiming itself a corner of Olympus.
Movement on the second-floor terrace made her
focus more finely. The balustrade hid all but the
head and shoulders of the man, who seemed to be
speeding the length of the terrace and back, over
and over, propelled by a mad urgency. When finally he stopped and stared out toward her, she could
see him more clearly and the top of the wheelchair
in which he sat. She flinched from his gaze, then
realized he wasn't looking at the DiGiorgio boat
but at the *Lord Jim* moored farther out in the bay.
It was a forbidding, embittered face, quite ancient

and craggy, with a small rockslide on the right side. She felt she had seen it before, perhaps in a painting of one of the old masters, or an actor playing King Lear.

"How do you do, Mr. Savage," she said out loud. "I've been wanting to meet you for a long time. Like since yesterday morning." She studied the face but could catch no change of expression. The body was hunched forward, unmoving. It was a strong, unfinished face with a large well-formed nose, eyes that glittered in deep recesses under bristling brows, long straggly hair that fell over the right forehead. "What secrets are you hiding?" she asked him. "What ghosts are wailing in your skull?" She remembered Steve's mother saying that Savage Point was haunted. As Sally looked at James Cotton Savage, she felt she was looking at a man who was haunted . . . gazing fixedly at a boat that was haunted.

All summer long the dark, sleek boat had remained at anchor, looming like a specter over the smaller craft in the bay. Each winter, Walter Keller had told her, the *Lord Jim* was sailed farther out on Long Island to a boatyard where it was scraped, painted, and refitted to remain at anchor the following year. Was the old man grieving for his long-dead wife who had died on the boat? And was the boat now cast in the role of a mausoleum for the loved one? And were his visits to the terrace the equivalent of placing fresh flowers on the grave? "Are you the last of the great romantics, Mr. Savage?" Her eyes blurred, and she brusquely wiped them.

When she looked back, he had changed position.

He was sitting upright, gazing at the clouds overhead. There was no mistaking the arrogance in his posture. He raised his right arm and shook his fist, then whirled the wheelchair and disappeared through the French doors. For seconds Sally continued to stare at the empty stage, not wanting the scene to end. The pantomime had been a complete mystery to her, but she was moved.

She lowered the glasses a fraction of an inch. Virginia Goldsboro stood on the top step of the porch below the terrace, her legs apart, her arms akimbo. How long she had been there, Sally didn't know. Still in the romantic mood, Sally tried to read the woman's stance. There was pride there but no arrogance, a contentment, a look of proprietorship in what she saw. Sally thought she read some sadness there, too, then laughed at her attempts to interpret Virginia Goldsboro's body language when the woman was probably just checking out the weather. Her gaze wasn't fixed on one point, like that of the man in the wheelchair, but encompassed the whole seascape from her own grounds to the distant Throgs Neck Bridge. There was one odd thing about her: she was wearing glasses. Again, Sally was touched, guessing at the vanity of the nearsighted woman who never wore glasses when others were around because she didn't want to look schoolmarmish. A moment later, Virginia Goldsboro went down the steps and around the house, taking off her glasses as she went, probably to her car, which she would drive without her glasses. This was a dangerous woman, Sally thought, behind the wheel of a car.

The transistor radio had been with the binocu-

lars. She knew it was unwise to turn it on: sound
carries a remarkable distance over water. She
didn't really want to hear the news, it was sure to
be painful. Nevertheless she turned on WNEW at
low volume. A man was being funny about sports.
A commercial for *Time* magazine. Then, ''Here's
the latest on the search for Little Sally. She is still
missing, but the police believe she is hiding in the
vicinity of Savage Point where her husband,
Stephen Cochran, was killed by a shotgun blast
early yesterday morning. Correspondent Jerry
Blockman is with the man in charge of the search,
Captain Grogan of the 111th Precinct. Jerry.''

''Captain Grogan, why do you think Little Sally
is still in the area?''

''I can't tell you that, Jerry, other than to say
that she has been sighted there.''

''Captain, everyone is assuming that Little Sally
killed her husband. Did she confess?''

''No, Jerry, we didn't have a chance to interrogate her before she escaped.''

''Was she under arrest, Captain?''

''Her rights were read to her by one of the of-
ficers and, yes, Jerry, she was under arrest,
though we didn't have a chance to book her.''

''Why was she under arrest, Captain?''

''She was a material witness, Jerry. She was the
only one in the house at the time. We definitely
wanted to interrogate her.''

''But I've heard there's been an increase in
burglaries on Savage Point, Captain. Couldn't it
have been a burglar, who may have been surprised
by Mr. Cochran?''

''No, Jerry, we thought of that, but there was no

sign of a break-in, and all of the evidence points to Little Sally as the perpetrator. I might add that her fingerprints were found on the shotgun.''

''What motive have you uncovered, Captain?''

''We don't know for sure, Jerry. In cases like this, where there may be an unstable person involved, we sometimes never find out what sets them off, it could be a little thing, we may never know.''

''Can you tell us whether she's dangerous, Captain? Is she carrying any weapon?''

''No, no weapon that we know of, Jerry. As far as being dangerous, remember Little Sally's an athlete, and she has a history of mental illness.''

''One last question, Captain. When do you expect to pick her up?''

''It should be any hour now, Jerry.''

In a rage, Sally picked up the radio to throw it against the bulkhead. ''Unstable person! How stupid can you get?'' She restrained herself. The damaging part was the confirmation that her prints were on the gun. Saying dazedly to herself, ''Oh, Steve, I didn't do it, you know I didn't do it,'' she turned to WCBS, which was in the middle of its report.

''I really have nothing to say,'' a man was saying. ''I'm only trying to cooperate with the police, that's why I'm here at the police station. But I scarcely knew the poor woman. They tell me she acted strangely, but I haven't been a witness to that. All I know is that on Saturday night the Cochrans were quarreling. She pulled her husband from the Keller's party, and I heard her say, 'Your looks could kill.' ''

"What did she mean by that, Mr. Savage?"

Sally slumped on the bunk, trying to understand. Was Cousin Charles deliberately lying, or is that the way his besotted brain interpreted her innocent comment? He wasn't drunk now. His voice came over as firm and convincing. It didn't sound like Cousin Charles at all. The next voice she heard, however, was painfully familiar.

"Sally, this is Pastor John. Hear me not only as your spiritual adviser but as your friend." The excessive warmth of the voice could burn out the radio, she thought. "Sally, there is nothing to be afraid of. Everybody on the point is your friend. If you are listening to my voice, Sally, I want you to give yourself up. Come out of wherever you are hiding, go up to the nice policeman and say, 'I am Sally Cochran, I believe you are looking for me.' Now will you do that?"

Sally mimicked, "I am Sally Cochran, I am a loony, take me away and lock me up." The preposterous voice of the minister sounded so funny to her that her self-doubts vanished. The whole world is crazy, she announced to herself, and I'm the only sane one left.

Another voice was now speaking with a vague Middle-European accent. "Can only speak theoretically. I have not interviewed her. But the pattern is quite classic. The person who kills two husbands is really killing her father over and over again. It is the father she hates, not the men she married. But, don't you see, each man, when she marries him, *becomes* her father. If the pattern holds in this case, and I venture to say it does, we'll find that Little Sally's father was a stern man who tried to suppress the natural instincts in his daughter, particularly at the time of puberty—"

Sally turned it off. Even the psychiatrists were mad. At the time of my puberty, Herr Doktor, she said, my stern father was long dead and my stern Uncle Joe was so hateful that he twisted himself right around my little finger. Dear Uncle Joe. Her mood was almost merry as she faced the long period of waiting until 1:30.

THE WAITING BECAME INTOLERABLE. She took her crumpled clothes out of the mesh bag, carefully laid them out straight on the bunk beneath the mattress, put the mattress back in place, and sat on it. She washed and groomed herself several times. She tried to concentrate on Steve's murder, but couldn't. Forgive me, Steve. She didn't risk turning on the radio again. She did risk the binoculars, however, a small risk since only the two round disks of the lenses would show at the bottom of the curtain. Through the starboard window she scanned Savage Point for a long time without seeing much activity: an occasional police car, a few passenger cars, delivery vans.

Moving to the port side, she studied the alien shores of Bayside, the hypnotic flow of traffic on the Cross Island, the fascinating dearth of activity at the Bayside marina, finally focusing on the *Lord Jim*. It was truly a handsome boat, long and graceful, one that would delight the eye if it weren't for the somber charcoal coat. A skull-and-crossbones should fly from its mast, she thought, not to indicate a pirate ship but a floating sepulcher. She scanned its length, tried to see into its ports, a

mystery ship, a modern *Mary Celeste*, deserted.
What awful thing had happened aboard? Was the
food still on the table, the coffee still hot on the
stove?

A blurred image intruded on her field of vision.
It blotted out the *Lord Jim*. Sally became rigid. It
appeared to be a giant face, or rather a portion of a
face, and its eye seemed to be looking right at her.
Her instinct was to pull the binoculars away from
the window. Her reason told her that a boat had
moved between her and the *Lord Jim*, but she
couldn't tell how far away it was or whether there
were other eyes inspecting the DiGiorgio boat at
this moment. Fearful that a slight flutter of the
curtain might invite closer inspection, she held the
binoculars in place, trying not to move them. The
image moved up and down, totally out of the field,
then back in. For a long time it was gone, all she
could see was the *Lord Jim*, and she wondered if
the intruding boat had gone on its way. She didn't
dare move her own eyes away from the binocular
sights. Suddenly the *Lord Jim* was replaced in the
lenses by a gigantic blurred eye, and she heard
voices, male murmurs. Something thudded against
the side of the boat. Did it jar her into moving the
binoculars? She held her breath.

One voice said, "Satisfied, Hawk-Eye?"

The other said, "They still look like binoculars to
me."

"So they're binoculars. You wanna go in and
take a look?"

"Even if we checked it out yesterday, wise guy,
doesn't mean she can't be in there today."

The eye slid out of sight, and Sally suddenly

recalled that she had once again messed up the
cabin; moreover, there was no way she could affix
the binoculars in place while she scooted to a
hiding place. Getting caught in the pose of a peeping Tom, with her eyes to the window, was prefer-
able to hiding in that awful head, anyway. Two
minutes in there with the door closed would make
her a screaming maniac.

A third voice, with a rumble of authority, said,
"Here, bright boy, take a look at the buttons.
They're all snapped in tight. Somebody in there
could button himself in, yeah, all except the last
one. Have you ever tried it? There's no way he
could snap that last one from inside. Do you still
think our party's in there?"

"We—ell...."

"Course not, Chief!"

"Let's get moving."

She held the binoculars in place long after they
had left. Then she had some more peanut butter
and jelly.

1:45. THE GENTLE THUMP of Joey's boat against
the cabin cruiser did not startle her. It outraged
her. He had kept her waiting for fifteen minutes,
during which she had imagined wild and terrible
things. His delay was absolutely inexcusable.
When he finally slithered through the canvas flap,
however, she had her anger under control.

He looked at her with those dark concerned eyes
for a moment. "You okay?" he asked.

She nodded, feeling inexplicably weepy.

He said, "They're looking for a teenager." She
grunted and sat down on the bunk. "They know

about the school jacket and the T-shirt and the jeans. It felt funny to hear them describe my clothes on you. They didn't mention the hair.''

Boomer, she thought, it had to be Boomer. He had said Savage Point people don't get involved, and she had believed him. So it wasn't Boomer himself. But he would have told Walter Keller and probably the Savages. Bingo: Cousin Charles. The tub of lard seemed to be carrying the ball for the family against her. Oh, well, she concluded miserably.

"I brought you this." Joey held out the *Daily News*. From across the cabin, she could see the picture of her in leotards and the block headline, ''Little Sally Flees Murder Rap.'' She limply held out her hand.

"And this," Joey said. In his other hand he held out a furry thing, and for a moment she thought he had brought her another wounded animal. Then she saw it was a wig. ''My mother says you can use it," he said.

"Oh, it's darling,'' she said, starting to laugh giddily. It was a frosted wig, with tight curls, intended to accompany an evening gown. "It'll make me look like George Washington," she said, and instead of laughing she was crying. Oh, wow, she said to herself, my nerves are in a terrible state. She apologized to Joey. "I love it. I'm crying because I love it."

When she had composed herself, Joey made her try it on, helping her straighten it like an anxious hairdresser. She looked at herself in the mirror. "By George," she said, "right off a dollar bill.... Joey, this makes me look ridiculous.''

"My mother, too," he said.

"Really, I couldn't be seen in public like this."

"Look again," he said. "Do you look like Mrs. Cochran? Or somebody else?"

She didn't want to say what she looked like for fear of insulting Joey's mother in front of him. She agreed that she didn't look like Sally Cochran, and certainly not like Little Sally. She looked like the sort of person the real Sally Cochran would turn her eyes away from. Maybe others would have the same reaction. "Joey DiGiorgio, you're a master of disguise," she said.

She forced herself to read the *Daily News* stories, including one by the sports editor and a long rehash of the Willie Spencer case. There were more pictures of herself in leotards and a terrible one of a haggard Sally being taken to the hospital. "Hey, Nino, do you know I om hoff Sponeesh?" she said, trying to imitate a Puerto Rican accent. "It say so here. I deedn't know that."

"Aren't you half Spanish?" Joey asked.

"Sure. But the implication here is that the meexed blood make me loco in the coco. I no crazy lady, *mi muchacho*."

The only Savage Point residents mentioned in the *News* stories were Walter Keller, because he was Little Sally's lawyer, and Charles Savage, because he supplied a hint of a motive—the Cochrans were quarreling. Walter Keller said he had no comment. In another development, the police in Mobile, Alabama, had been alerted to look for her in the event she had eluded the Savage Point dragnet and had headed for her hometown. Three unverified sightings were reported in Mobile.

And there was a quote from the slain man's mother, Mrs. Michael Cochran, of Mamaroneck. "My daughter-in-law did not kill my son," the *News* quoted her as saying. "Savage Point killed my son." The paper described her as distraught.

Sally's thoughts suddenly went back to Joey's original announcement. "That policeman who saw me last night," she said, "Did he come back?"

Joey was sitting on the step in the doorway, his elbows on his knees, his long hands dangling. He nodded. "Pop went out of town and I was at school. They tried to give Mom a hard time, but that dumb cop never took a good look at you. Mom told them you were my cousin Angelina from Brooklyn, and they bought it. So there's nothing to worry about."

"How about Angelina?"

"It's okay. She'll give them a straight story."

"I'm sorry to have caused this trouble for your family."

"No trouble. It's what we had to do."

"You're the crazy ones," she said, "and I love you for it."

"I told mom she should've said you were my girl friend from school. I would've liked that better." His face was reddening, but this time his deep brown eyes did not turn away from hers. His mouth was curved in a tentative smile.

"I would have liked that, too," she said. "Do you have a girl friend?"

"Not right now. Girls scare me."

"And I don't?" she said.

"Oh, gee, yes, you do. But—" He seemed unable to put his elusive feelings into words. She realized she was being made love to by a fifteen-year-old boy, and her unsteady emotions led her a jagged path of rises and falls, from gratitude to love to hilarity to sadness to dumb yearning to remembrance of the touch of Steve to guilt to despair and back to gratitude, as Joey finished his sentence. "Well, you're different."

She couldn't think of anything else to say but, "Thank you." What she felt for Joey was *sisterly* love, she thought; they were two simpatico people, that's all. Yet her tangle of emotions was bringing tears to her eyes. Easy does it, sister, she said to herself. Aloud, she said, "When I was your age, I was scared silly of boys."

"Really? I can't believe it!" he said, and they both laughed.

She said, "Okay, Mr. Disguise Artist. What should I wear?"

He said, "You can't wear the blue dress, and you can't be a teenager. And none of my mom's clothes'd fit you. What do you have left?" She showed him the tan blouse and brown skirt. "Oh, yeah," he said. "Has anybody seen you in that getup?"

"No."

"Okay. Then put it on."

She started to take off the T-shirt. "I'm going to miss this old shirt," she said. Joey remained sitting on the step, watching her. Her own reactions annoyed her. She said, rather sharply, "Maybe you better turn your back."

An uncertain smile tilted a corner of his mouth.

"How about if I only half close my eyes?" He squinted. "Like this."

She tried to repress a laugh, and failed. She tried to speak sternly. "No go, Joey. Brothers don't peek at their sisters."

He said, "I don't have a sister," a little sulkily, and he turned his body so that he was looking away from her.

She quickly slipped out of the shirt and jeans. "Goodbye, lovely shirt," she said, wishing to let him know how much she appreciated his clothing. "Goodbye, lovely jeans." Standing in her bra and Joey's shorts, she glanced at him, followed his gaze to a polished brass plaque she hadn't noticed before on the wall between windows; she saw his face in it looking at her, distorted but quite clear. Heaven only knew what the funny mirror was doing to her figure as he saw it through the brass, she thought; it certainly couldn't be very attractive. She was about to chide him, and stopped. What the hell.

She hastily put on her blouse, pulled up the zipper, slipped the skirt over her head and tugged it down into place; the zipper sounded a note of finality. "Okay, Mr. Peeping Tom," she said, "the show is over."

He slowly turned back to her, with an embarrassed smile on his face. He said, "Er, when's the next show?"

"It closed Saturday night," she said. Then, remembering the horrible final act of Saturday night, she added, "Go, get yourself a girl friend." Sharper than she intended.

The question of her next step was already solved

in her mind. According to the *News*, Steve's mother didn't blame her for Steve's death. Consequently, Sally didn't have to worry about getting a hostile reception from her mother-in-law, provided she could get through to her. "Since you're the miracle worker, Joey," she said, "get me to Mamaroneck."

When he looked at her questioningly, she said, "If you can just get me to the Bayside marina, I can walk on down and get the train." He still looked blank. She said, "Don't you see, it's important that I talk to my husband's mother. She may know why someone'd want to kill him."

He said, "Going by train would take you all day. I have a better idea." He stood up. In the enclosure of the cabin, he seemed much taller, almost a man. "My Laser is outside," he said. "I'll sail you over to Bayside, and then we'll pick you up in the car. It'll be much quicker."

"We?"

"My mom and me."

Sally protested, but he easily overrode her objections; after all, the car did make more sense than the roundabout rail route. She said, "Are you sure your mother will drive us?"

He said, "She doesn't drive. I do." Sally started to protest again. He said, "I'm taking driver's ed. I have my permit. Do you have a license?" She said yes, and he said, "Good. You'll sit next to me." Neither of them gave a thought to the name on the license. He had been moving closer as he spoke. He was about six inches from her. He said, "Would you be mad if I, sort of, hugged you? I really want to."

She said, "Aw, come on, Joey. The show is over, remember?"

"I know. I just want to hug you, that's all."

She held out her arms, saying, "Oh, Joey." He put his arms around her and held her close. Her emotions were as tremulous as his, mixed with a little exasperation. It was a sweet embrace, and she didn't wish to break it, but it wasn't completely sisterly. She stirred, and he slowly pulled away. "Thank you," he said. "I've been wanting to do that." She needed arms around her, even if they were a fifteen-year-old boy's. He said, "You're a very nice person, Mrs. Cochran." She said, "You're pretty nice yourself, Mr. DiGiorgio."

He turned away, suddenly brusque. "I think we better go now. I'm sorry you're gonna get wet. The water's a little rough."

WITH THE WIND BLOWING STEADILY from the northeast, he maintained the little sailboat on a constant starboard tack, past the *Lord Jim*, across the open water. She crouched in an unrecognizable ball in the rear, unable to look at either shore or watch for craft heading their way. She had put the wig and shoes in the mesh bag to keep them dry; her right side was soaked from the spray. A sudden gust nearly capsized them, but she instinctively leaned to starboard as he tacked further into the wind.

Approaching the marina dock, she got out the wig and shoes, and put them on. There was little activity at the marina, just a few men doing mysterious things with hoses, dismantled masts, an outboard motor on a block. She clambered to the float, as Joey steadied the bouncing Laser. He said loudly, "We'll pick you up in a little while, mother." No one was paying attention.

SHE SAT ON THE BENCH, feeling terribly conspicuous. The wind was chill on her wet clothes, but she didn't dare to put on the blue sweater. Joggers went by, in deep communion with their own jouncing flesh. She was the only bench-sitter in the marina grounds. It's a wonder the police don't pick her up as a derelict or a suicidal eccentric intent on freezing to death, she thought. Shivering, she hugged her misery to her breasts.

She didn't know what she had expected, perhaps a nondescript car of some sort, but the gleaming, baby-blue Cadillac surprised her. Of course, it was Johnny Dee's car and she had seen it occasionally on Dover Road, but she hadn't associated gentle Joey with such an ostentatious monster.

Gemma DiGiorgio struggled out of the front seat, waved to Sally, saying, "Come on," and she climbed into the backseat, leaving the front one for Sally. Joey looked different, more grown-up in a jacket, shirt and tie; even so, he looked too young to be behind the wheel of a Cadillac. He pointed to a jacket on the seat. "Put this on. You're shivering."

"Another one of yours?" she asked.

"No, mom's, before she started eating too much pasta."

His mother said, "Don't be fresh, Joey." To Sally, she said, "Turn around, Mrs. Cochran." After studying the wig a moment, she said, "So that's what I looked like. You can keep it, Mrs.

Cochran." To the world in general, she said, "Well, is it going to rain, or isn't it?"

They discussed the weather for a minute, while Joey steered the huge car back onto the Cross Island, heading for the Throgs Neck Bridge. Ahead of him was a slow-moving Buick with an old man at the wheel. Joey flicked on the turn signal preparatory to switching lanes in order to pass. His mother said, "Don't show off, Joey." He slumped just a little and canceled the signal. "He has to be careful," she said to Sally. "He don't have a real license yet."

Sally said, "I know. I think he's doing masterfully." Hearing the patronizing word, she said to Joey, "You're doing great. When's the next show?" They partially glanced at each other and grinned.

At the toll booth, Joey yelled in panic, "Who's got seventy-five cents?" He was in an exact-change line.

Sally said, "Sorry, not me."

Mrs. DiGiorgio said, "I left my pocketbook home, what d'ya think of that?"

Joey said, "Damn. I wanted to stay away from the booths."

His mother said, "Watch your language."

Since most people hate Cadillac drivers, Joey had a hard time switching into the next lane. Sally handed him a dollar. She slunk down in her seat, then realized it made her look like a dwarf, so she sat up straight, her face turned away from the toll collector. The attendant in the next booth, just a few feet away from her, had his back to her. Scotch-taped to the window beside him was the

front page of the *Daily News* with her picture on
it. Joey tapped her on the shoulder and said, "He
wants you to turn this way, mother." She turned,
scowling. The attendant said, "Thank you,
mother. Sorry to bother you."

Accelerating from the booth, Joey said, "Hot
damn, that was close."

His mother said, "Joey!"

Sally said. "Lucky they weren't looking for
George Washington," then bit her tongue.

At the next toll booth, Joey, believing the toll
would be a quarter, again got on the exact-change
line, only to find that the toll was thirty cents. He
switched lines again, sweating and swearing.

Gemma said, "Joey!"

He turned off at the Mamaroneck Road exit.
Sally said, "Find the railroad station. I know the
way from there."

4:21. JOEY ROLLED SLOWLY past the garden apartment. They could see no sign of surveillance. He
pulled into an off-street parking area, berthed his
baby-blue ship in a space marked Ziegler. "What'll
I do if Ziggy shows up?" he asked.

Gemma reached over the seat, touched Sally's
shoulder. "I think it'd be best if we went together,
Mrs. Cochran." When Sally looked puzzled, she
said, "You know. Two old broads visiting a neighbor. They won't be looking for two gabby old
dames, just one scared little acrobat. Joey'll stay
with the car."

Sally said, "You're as smart as Mr. Genius here.
Let's go."

Joey said, "What if she isn't home?"

What if the police are in the apartment with her, Sally wondered. The small lobby was protected by a speaker system. She would have to identify herself into the speaker, not knowing whether Bess was alone or not. When Bess's voice inquired tinnily, "Who is it?" Sally grimaced at Gemma.

"Hi, Bess, surprise, surprise!" she said. "It's Barney Harper's little old cousin-in-law, that's who it is." The "Bess" was the identifying word; Steve was the only one who ever called her that.

The voice said uncertainly, "Sally?"

"Hey, are you alone? I don't want to walk into a crowd of people, or butt in on anything."

The voice said, "Come on up," and the door buzzed. Sally still didn't know what awaited her. "We'll soon find out," she said, leading Gemma up the stairs.

Steve's mother was inside the open doorway, dressed in funereal garb, different navy colors that clashed, probably the only somber things in her wardrobe. They stared at each other for a long moment. The once-lovely, once-jolly cartoon face was a grief-stricken caricature; the eyes were red and swollen; the blotches on the round cheeks looked red and swollen, too. Sally had never felt close to Steve's mother: the only thing they had in common was Steve—at different periods of his life. But at the sight of her now, Sally wailed, "Oh, Bess," and rushed to embrace her, sobbing.

Bess seemed embarrassed. She held Sally off, saying, "Whatever in the world are you doing in that thing? You're a sight. Introduce me to your friend."

Gemma insisted on staying in the kitchen. She

made the instant coffee, served it and retreated to the kitchen. Bess Cochran said, "Take that thing off, child. I feel as if I'm talking to a stranger." Sally took off the wig, and Bess said, "Oh, your lovely hair. What a shame." She sat in a straight-backed chair, ill at ease. Sally sat on the edge of a stuffed chair.

Sally blurted, "Oh, mom, you look awful. I'm so terribly sorry."

"You don't look so hot yourself," Bess said.

"I loved Steve very much. He was—he was—"

"I'm sure you did, child," Bess said. "Did you kill him?"

"No."

"I didn't think you did. Steve was a better judge of people than that. The undertaker is down in the city getting him now. They tell me he was shot in the face."

"Don't look at him, mother."

"I don't think I could stand it. He had such a fine face. Just like his father. I don't think I could stand it. Tell me what happened."

Sally told her, omitting as much of the horror as she could. Even so, the cartoon face took on a clenched look. "And all the doors were locked," Bess said. Sally said, "Yes." "The windows?" "The bedroom window was open. They'd have had to use a ladder to get in that way. There was no ladder."

Suddenly the clownish face cast words at her. "I told you to stay away from Savage Point."

Sally said, "It was Steve's idea. I only went along."

"You should have stopped him," Bess said,

rocking slightly in her chair. "You should have stopped him." She lapsed into silence, looking into her lap.

"Mother," Sally said. Getting no reaction, she said, "Bess." The older woman looked at her. "You lived there thirty years ago."

"You found out about that."

"In the house next door to Greystone."

"I don't want to talk about it."

In grim exasperation, Sally said, "Someone killed your son. Someone on Savage Point. They blasted his lovely face with a shotgun. Don't you want to find out who did it?"

"Savage Point!"

"The whole community didn't do it, Bess. One person did it. There had to be a reason. I think it goes back to thirty years ago when you and Mike lived there. Something happened."

Bess fidgeted, squirmed. "Don't you think I've thought it all over? I've been doing nothing else for the last twenty-four hours. Yes, something happened, but for the life of me I can't think why anyone would want to—" She put her hand to her mouth as a sob heaved her body.

Sally went to her, put her hand on her shoulder in sympathy. "You're going to have to tell me, mom. You kept it from Steve, so it was something you didn't want him to know. But it can't hurt him now. Start at the beginning. You and Mike."

"Me and Mike."

"Was it something Mike did?"

"Mike?"

Impatiently, Sally said, "Did Mike Cochran do something disgraceful? Is that what it was?"

Bess Cochran frowned. "Oh, Mike wouldn't do anything disgraceful. Except get drunk now and then. He had the curse of the Irish. He was a drinker."

Sally went back to her chair. "Tell me about Mike," she said.

"Mike Cochran was a fine man," Bess said. "He deserved better. But maybe he shouldn't've married. He liked sports and he liked the company of men around a bar. He liked to be laughing all the time. He was thirty-five and I was twenty-one when we married. What do you want to know?"

"About Mike. Why do you say he shouldn't have married?"

Bess sighed. "You know how some men are born bachelors. Well, dear Mike worshiped women like he did the Virgin Mary, but he was afraid of them. I was too young to know any better, maybe I could have helped him. I was a pretty young thing. Would you believe I was ever pretty? And I guess you could say I was spirited, always kicking up my heels. I loved dancing—oh, I was a fine dancer— and ice-skating and swimming and flirting. I was a terrible flirt, and the men knew it was just innocent fun. Except Mike. When I flirted with my husband, I think he became frightened. Of what, I don't know. And he drank. After a while we didn't get along too well."

Sally ended a moment of silence, by asking, "When did you move to Savage Point?"

"What? Oh, I remember it well. It was the fall of 1948. It was Mike's idea, I liked it where we were in Bayside, but he had spent part of his childhood on the point, and it *is* a great area for kids, isn't it?

We were going to try seriously for a family. I was twenty-eight and not getting any younger. We knew something was wrong, so we went to the doctors and we found out it was Mike's fault. I shouldn't use that word, he couldn't help it. But I think that was Mike's crowning blow, on top of being rejected during the war. He would have done anything to get in. World War Two was made for the likes of Mike. He had some sort of a pocket in his intestines and when he got these stomach attacks of his he had to watch his diet, that's all, but it was enough to keep him out. I shouldn't be telling you all this, it has nothing to do with the price of coffee. As I say, Mike was a fine man." She stopped talking.

"Tell me about you and Mike on Savage Point," Sally prompted her.

Bess jumped up. "Have some more coffee," she said.

"No, thank you."

"I'll get some for your friend in the kitchen."

"She can get it for herself."

"Are you sure now?"

"Bess!"

Bess sighed and sat down. "Here we were, the two of us, in that big house. Mike kept going on business trips and, even when he didn't, he often wouldn't come home from work, saying he had to work late. He'd just bunk down at the office or go to a hotel or something. It wasn't other women. It was just that it was hard for him to face me, I guess. And he couldn't stand his old drinking buddies because they were always talking about what happened to them in the war. That was a terrible,

dreary winter. When I'd go out with our old
friends from Bayside, it wasn't the same without
Mike. But that's neither here nor there.

"I decided to get busy and stay busy and stop
feeling sorry for myself. I started playing tennis at
the club, and went to club affairs. I joined the
beautification committee of the civic association,
and I joined the fleet and all that. One of Mike's
uncles was handy to escort me. And I'd occasionally bump into James Cotton Savage and his sister,
Alice. He was very good at everything, tennis,
swimming, boating, and she was involved in
everything else. The first time I was in Greystone
was at a beautification committee meeting, which
Alice was the head of. She wasn't living there, you
understand, but she used it like it was hers. Cotton's wife was, how shall I say it, standoffish,
always with a sour expression on her face. I
thought of her as a frozen puss. Anyway, I didn't
like the place, too big and cold, but what does that
have to do with anything?

"The only other time I was at Greystone was at a
party. The invitation came to Mike and me, but he
wouldn't go. He said there was a feud between the
families. Of course, the feud, as he called it, didn't
stop Mike's uncle from escorting me, so it was just
something in Mike's head. It was a really glorious
evening in May, I remember, and the party spilled
out of the ballroom—I always thought of it as a
ballroom, anyway—and onto the grand porch. The
sunset was spectacular, the music was romantic,
and I danced with Cotton Savage. He was a handsome man, tall, trim, his hair was gray at the
temples, and he danced like a god. I flirted with

him, and he seemed to be delighted. And that was that.'' Bess's thick body seemed to be swaying to the remembered music, and her round face had a little smile on it; and Sally caught a small glimpse of the tantalizing young woman she must have been.

The older woman had stopped talking again. Sally said, ''That was that. Is that all?''

Bess lowered her eyes. ''Not exactly.''

Suddenly, Sally knew what Bess had kept from her son and was trying to avoid saying to her daughter-in-law. ''You had an affair with him, didn't you?''

Bess looked at her with wounded eyes. ''That's a pretty blunt way of putting it. Makes it sound tawdry. We fell in love, it's that simple. And that glorious. Oh, not then. Nothing happened at the party. It ended, and I thought that was that. Then one evening I was at the bedroom window looking at the sunset and cursing Greystone for ruining the view, when he appeared at his window and waved.''

''Which one was it? The double window at the left?''

''You've seen it. Yes, that window. I waved back. Then he imitated the waltz we had danced at the party, holding his hands out as if I were in them, then he bowed to me. I don't know what I did, I think I did a silly Irish jig. Then I blew him a kiss. And that was that. We were both laughing.

''Mike and I still had our little boat that we'd had at Bayside. They didn't start the launch service till near the end of June. Do they still wait so late? It seems an awful waste of June. Anyway, it was one of the first days of the service, Cotton and I got on the same launch run. Our mooring was pretty far out, right near the *Lord Jim.* So we had a chance to talk together, and I said he had a lovely boat. I imitated Katharine Hepburn in *The Philadelphia Story.* I said it was 'yar,' not sure what it meant. He asked if I wanted to see it, and I said yes. And that was that.

"I won't describe it for you, it doesn't matter. Let me just say it was the most magnificent boat I could imagine. All shiny mahogany and brass, and a big covered deck where he did his entertaining, and a master stateroom with thick carpeting on the floor. He put some Strauss on the Victrola and we danced. All by ourselves. We were dancing on water, but it was like dancing on air. Every time he had to change the record he bowed to me and I curtsied back and we laughed. He had some chilled wine on board, and we talked. He had been in the war, a captain of some ship or other, but he wouldn't talk about that. His wife wasn't well, but he wouldn't talk about that, either. I didn't talk about Mike, it wouldn't have been proper. But he knew I was lonely and I knew he was lonely, just from the way we looked at each other. Oh, it was sad and romantic, just like in a Charles Boyer movie, only he looked more like Gary Cooper. Then he showed me the bedroom, and that was that, and I'm not going into *that.*" She glared defiantly at Sally, as if Sally had asked her to describe the lovemaking. Sally was in a mood to believe it was tender and passionate, gentle and ecstatic, emotional and forever.

Unexpectedly, Bess giggled. "Do you know how

we sent signals to each other? Flowers in the window! When the coast was clear, we put flowers there, and when it was clear for both of us, we met on the *Lord Jim* at nine. We wouldn't go on the same launch. I'd go out to our boat and then slip into the water and swim over. We did that all summer long, and nobody ever knew! The only one who might have suspected was the driver of the launch, a young red-headed boy, but he never said anything. I didn't like the way he looked at me, that's all.

"To some people that might sound sneaky, but it wasn't that way at all. It was just that we had to be discreet. You know Savage Point. There were rules of conduct that you didn't break. You never gave cause for scandal, and Cotton, as the founder of the community practically, and the head of the church practically, couldn't possibly let himself be caught in a scandal. People didn't take divorce so easily then. Oh, we talked and talked and I would have been happy to divorce Mike, but Cotton was married to a minister's daughter and she was mentally ill besides going through a long menopause. Do you know they hadn't been to bed together for three years? I know I shouldn't talk about that, but I think that woman treated him abominably! I didn't cry when she died. And to think that it was only six months after Mike and I moved out that she had her heart attack, and Cotton would have been free to marry me! Only six months!"

"What happened, Bess?"

"I got pregnant."

Out of the sudden whirl of thoughts in her head,

out of their roar, Sally voiced the most outrageous one. "Steve?"

Bess was crying quietly. She nodded her head.

Sally tried to order her thoughts, but something kept insisting, "The Savage connection!" Steve was the illegitimate son of James Cotton Savage. "The Savage Connection!" There had been fornication in the city of God, and the harlot had been cast outside the walls, where they were to be stoned to death, both the adulteress and the misbegotten product of the illicit congress. And having escaped the stoning at birth by moving unto the land of Mamaroneck, was the grown outcast still subject to an Old Testament sentence of death and damnation? Steve, not knowing his terrible heritage, blithely returned to the domain of his ordained executioner for the final ceremony. Is that the way it was?

No, it doesn't make any sense at all. Only a mad person would consider himself God's executioner and, if he were to eliminate every bastard on earth, he would decimate the human race. No, there had to be a reason, either cold or passionate, for Steve's murder. By returning unknowingly to the scene of his origin, he may well have been a walking embarrassment to the family, a bar sinister on their glistening shield, that roused feelings of animosity and a wish that he were dead. But for someone to act on that wish by blowing the intruder's head off? Not in civilized Savage Point.

Crying, Bess said, "No one knew. Oh, Sally, I feel terrible telling you this, you're the first one I've ever told it to, and all for nothing, I'm afraid. I can't see what it has to do with my baby's death."

1. How do you rate _____ ?
   (Please print book TITLE)

   1.6 ☐ excellent .4 ☐ good .2 ☐ not so good
   .5 ☐ very good .3 ☐ fair .1 ☐ poor

2. How likely are you to purchase another book in this series?
   2.1 ☐ definitely would purchase .3 ☐ probably would not purchase
   .2 ☐ probably would purchase .4 ☐ definitely would not purchase

3. How do you compare this title with similar books you usually read?
   3.1 ☐ far better than others .4 ☐ not as good
   .2 ☐ better than others .5 ☐ definitely not as good
   .3 ☐ about the same

4. Have you any additional comments about this book?
   _____ (4)
   _____ (6)

5. How did you first become aware of this book?
   8. ☐ in-store display 11. ☐ talk show
   9. ☐ radio 12. ☐ read other titles
   10. ☐ magazine _____ 13. ☐ other _____
   (name) (please specify)

6. What most prompted you to buy this book?
   14. ☐ title 17. ☐ picture on cover 20. ☐ back-cover story outline
   15. ☐ price 18. ☐ friend's recommendation 21. ☐ read a few pages
   16. ☐ author 19. ☐ product advertising 22. ☐ other _____
   (please specify)

7. How do you usually obtain your books?
   23. ☐ bookstore 26. ☐ department/discount store 29. ☐ borrow
   24. ☐ drugstore 27. ☐ convenience store 30. ☐ other
   25. ☐ supermarket 28. ☐ subscription
   (please specify)

8. What type(s) of paperback fiction have you purchased in the past 3 months? Approximately how many?

	No. purchased		No. purchased
☐ contemporary romance	(31)____	☐ espionage	(45)____
☐ historical romance	(33)____	☐ western	(47)____
☐ gothic romance	(35)____	☐ contemporary novels	(49)____
☐ romantic suspence	(37)____	☐ historical novels	(51)____
☐ mystery	(39)____	☐ science fiction/fantasy	(53)____
☐ private eye	(41)____	☐ occult	(55)____
☐ action/adventure	(43)____	☐ other	(57)____

9. On which date was this book purchased? (59) _____

10. Please indicate your age group and sex.
    61.1 ☐ Male 62.1 ☐ under 15 .3 ☐ 25-34 .5 ☐ 50-64
    .2 ☐ Female .2 ☐ 15-24 .4 ☐ 35-49 .6 ☐ 65 or older

Thank you for completing and returning this questionnaire.

NAME _____
(Please Print)

ADDRESS _____

CITY _____

ZIP CODE _____

BUSINESS REPLY MAIL

FIRST CLASS	PERMIT NO. 70	TEMPE, AZ.

POSTAGE WILL BE PAID BY ADDRESSEE

NATIONAL READER SURVEYS

1440 SOUTH PRIEST DRIVE
TEMPE, AZ. 85281

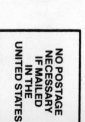

NO POSTAGE
NECESSARY
IF MAILED
IN THE
UNITED STATES

Sally went to her, knelt by the chair, put her arms around her waist. "I'm glad you told me," she said. She almost said, "You should've told Steve long ago," but held back the words. She said, "It's not all for nothing, mom. I don't know exactly how, but it's important, all of it. Please, please finish the story."

After a while, Bess said in a controlled voice, "Might as well." Sally eased back into her own chair as the older woman continued. "It wasn't until October that I knew I was pregnant. I'd missed my period in September, but I was so giddy I didn't think much of it. The launch service ended, and Cotton and I didn't know what to do. We were actually talking about an apartment in Bay-side—can you believe it—as a meeting place for the winter. It wouldn't've worked. The *Lord Jim* was the heart of our romance. It had an other-worldly atmosphere. An apartment, no matter how nice, would've brought us down to earth, and we would have felt like what others would've called us, cheaters! I didn't think that at the time, and I'm so glad our love didn't go pale and die in an apartment. My memories of it are still grand and glorious.

"When I told Cotton the bad news—how can I call Steve bad news—he grew so sad I idiotically thought he was going to die. But men don't die of a broken heart, do they?"

"No, they live with it," Sally said, remembering the wreck of a man on Greystone's terrace.

"There's not much else to tell," Bess said. "As I say, I'd've divorced Mike in a minute if Cotton were willing, but when he tried to talk to Edith about it, he found that he couldn't. It was sort of like the Prince of Wales and Wallis Simpson, only Cotton didn't abdicate. And that was that. I thought it wouldn't be right to continue living next door to him with his child, and he agreed. He bought the house from us at a generous price, and gave it to the church. I always thought of it as an act of contrition, but maybe I'm wrong. I didn't know Cotton all that well. I know that he loved me, he wasn't lying about that, and that he grieved when he sent me away.

"Mike was another matter. He wasn't stupid. He knew the child wasn't his, and when Cotton bought the house he suspected it was Cotton's, but he wasn't sure. You see, that was the point, child, nobody knew! That's why I can't imagine this having anything to do with my baby's death. Anyway, poor Mike didn't know what to do. He hardly said another word to me. He went through the move to Mamaroneck, not knowing whether he should beat me, kill me, throw me out or what. He came and went, not saying anything. Finally, when I went into labor, he drove me to the hospital. That's the last I ever saw of him."

"He ran away?"

"I never heard from him again. I don't know where he went, or where he is, or even if he's still living. I don't hold it against him. I treated him very badly."

"But you didn't have any money, did you?"

"No, Mike took everything. I took a chance and called Cotton on the phone. He paid all the bills, and then he sent me a check for four hundred dollars every month until Steve graduated from law school. I expected it to stop then, but it didn't. He still sends me four hundred dollars every month. I like to think it's because he still loves me. It wasn't just for support of the child."

Sally thought it was a less-than-generous sum, but she didn't say so. She said, "Didn't Cotton's wife die around the same time?"

"I don't know exactly when," Bess said. "I didn't hear about it till months later—from Mike's uncle, not from Cotton. I never talked to Cotton again, but I kept up with Mike's uncle. After all, he had been my gallant escort and, besides, I liked him. He's not with us anymore, rest his soul." She sighed.

Sally leaned forward, said softly, "Why didn't you and Cotton get together again after you were both free?"

Bess looked at her with unseeing eyes as she searched for words. "There was no overpowering reason," she said. "Of course, I was still married to Mike, I never got a divorce from him, but that could've been easily fixed. And there could've been awkward questions in the community. My face was all broken out, and I looked a mess. But the main thing was, it was a beautiful thing that had happened between us, something that few human beings ever experience—and it was over. It was perfect, completed. There was no adding to it, or going back to it. That was that." The flat statement was like a book being slammed shut.

Sally looked at the middle-aged face and felt pity for the onetime flirt who had had three months of sublime passion and had sustained herself on the dry memory of it ever since. She said, "If he's been sending you checks every month for thirty years, mother, don't you think the family knows about them? They must have known who they were going to, and why."

"They may know about me, but not about Steve."

"I'll bet you're wrong," Sally said grimly. "And the launch attendant. Don't you think he might've put two and two together?"

"Now there was a sharp-eyed young man," Bess said. "He was only about fifteen or sixteen, but I don't think he missed a trick. He may have known we were meeting on the boat, but that's all."

"Do you remember his name?"

"I tried to think of that last night," Bess said. "All I can come up with is Kelly, something like that."

"Keller? Walter Keller?"

"It could be, child, I don't know."

Walter Keller again. The man who had unwittingly set up Steve's appointment with death now appears to have been in on his conception, the ferryman on the bay of love.

Sally asked more questions without getting any more information. Bess didn't recall meeting any of the other members of the Savage family, neither George Goldsboro nor the two kids, Virginia and Cousin Charles. When Bess hesitantly asked Sally if she had met Cotton Savage, Sally said no. It would have been cruel to describe the man on the terrace. She stood up to leave.

Bess said, "You're welcome to stay, child, but the police said they would come back. I'll show you where the stakeout is. Isn't that what they call them? Stakeouts?'' She led Sally to the front window, pointed to a black Pinto. It had appeared empty when Sally and Gemma had passed it earlier.

Sally said anxiously, ''You don't suppose they take pictures of everyone who comes in here?''

''I hope not, for your friend's sake,'' Bess replied. She watched Sally put on the wig, looked her up and down critically. ''Those blue shoes stick out like a sore thumb, child. What size do you wear?''

Sally left wearing a pair of Bess's brown shoes. She felt like a walking Salvation Army shop. At the door, they hugged each other warmly, almost fiercely. Bess said, ''You're in worse shape than I am, aren't you?'' Sally cried.

Sally and Gemma paused in the downstairs vestibule while Sally composed herself. At Gemma's suggestion, Sally walked closer to the Pinto, so she could face away from it and appear to be engrossed in talking to her friend. In fact, she was talking to Gemma, ''Can you see him? Is he looking at us? What's he doing now? Did you see him take any pictures? I think I'm going to trip in these shoes.'' Gemma said she hadn't seen any camera.

Joey was parked in a space marked Kilroy. ''Ziggy came back,'' he explained. Sally had a case of the shakes for the first five minutes of the trip back, while the DiGiorgios remained silent. Then she laughed, a little out of control.

She said to Joey, ''Remember we were trying to figure out the link between my husband and the Savage family?'' She turned to Gemma and said, ''You heard, didn't you?''

Gemma shrugged. "Couldn't help," she said.

Sally said to Joey, "Do you know what the link was? Steve was a Savage himself!" She laughed in the high registers.

Joey said uneasily, "That's funny."

Gemma said, "It's not that funny."

Sally apologized for her loss of control. Gemma said, "You're entitled. It's good to get it out. You got more coming. Make it loud. Nobody can hear. It's good for you." She said it in the same tones she had used in saying *mangia* last night.

Sally owed Joey a report; after a while, she was able to tell him the gist of her mother-in-law's story. "I know I don't have to say this," she said to the two of them. "But I'm going to say it just to make it official. This is her secret, and you're not to pass it along." Joey looked hurt. Gemma simply nodded. Sally added bitterly, "Of course, the killer must have known the secret, and maybe a lot of other people on Savage Point did, too. What a secret."

The toll-booth attendants on the return trip weren't quite so attentive to the search for Little Sally. No one was really expecting the quarry to run back into the trap. The three people in the blue Cadillac passed inspection without incident. In thinking back over Bess's story, Sally thought of a question she should have asked but didn't. Who was the doctor Bess went to when she found out she was pregnant?

8:05. SALLY CROUCHED in the thicket behind the Keller house. A half-fallen ailanthus gave her good cover in a shroud of weeds just a few yards beyond the dirt road. Lights were on in the living room and kitchen. She knew the punctual Kellers usually had dinner at 7:15, about twenty minutes after Walter got home. She envisioned Charlotte and one or another of the kids cleaning up in the kitchen. Despite the cloud cover, night had not yet settled in. She decided to wait; she would have only one opportunity to dash to the back porch across the lawn without being observed, and deeper darkness would give her a better chance. Her own house, next door, was hidden by the trees; an earlier glimpse had showed a dim light in the front hall. She knew it was staked out by the police, but she didn't know by how many. A cough and a momentary glow of a lighter placed one of them in the same copse with her, about a hundred feet away. She guessed he was the only one covering the rear.

Depositing her in the homeward-bound throng of commuters was Joey's idea. At 6:45 he boldly drove the gaudy car to the south side of the Savage Point railroad station, parked it with other cars waiting for the 6:20 out of Penn Station. Sally was nervous. Gemma DiGiorgio said, "Don't worry, Mrs. Cochran. We're just waiting for our fat-cat husbands to come home. Nobody expects you to be here."

She was quickly among the people trudging through the underpass to the north side where other cars were waiting. She saw Walter Keller ahead of her, and she slowed her pace. At the head of the stairs on the other side, she joined the trickle of people heading toward the houses in the swamp, past a police car parked in the turn-around. Her mesh bag was looped over her shoulder like some new-vogue handbag. She knew she looked strange but nothing at all like Little Sally. In the housing development, she split to the right and hastened, exposed, to the thicket of trees that stretched for several hundred feet to where she now hid back of the Kellers'. She changed to her teenage outfit because it was darker in hue and therefore better as camouflage, because she could run faster in Joey's sneakers, and because Walter Keller undoubtedly knew of her Cardozo disguise but not of the frosted wig. She was forced to trust him but only as far as was necessary.

Sometime after 8:30, Sally judged the night was dark enough for her to make her dash. Under the sound cover of a LaGuardia-bound jet, she flitted across the dirt road, raced to the house in the deeper darkness of the foliage at the far border of the Keller property, bounded up the stairs to the porch, and came to a standstill behind a pillar. She listened, heard nothing from behind her. The stereo was thumping at low volume upstairs in Sneaky Henry's room. She strode quickly to one of the two doors and opened it. Savage Point was an area where nobody locked his door at night, Walter Keller had told the Cochrans. Obviously, he believed it, even though that was before the burglaries had started.

The door she had chosen led into the large living room. A soft light on an end table revealed that the room was empty. She listened, heard Henry's stereo and the faint churring sound of a washing machine. She went to the entrance hall, through the dining room back to the kitchen. She found

Charlotte in the laundry room. Sally cleared her throat. "You have a visitor," she said.

Charlotte Keller turned and stared. "Well, *neighbor*!" she exclaimed. She glanced at the window, pulled Sally aside by the arm and flicked off the light behind her. "Stay here a moment while I get Walter. He's been wanting to talk to you." She disappeared.

Sally had an aversion to Charlotte, as disorganized people always do to others who are damnably efficient. Charlotte made her hundred-and-one daily chores look easy, and found time for wholesome pastimes, such as her painting and piano.

Walter said, "Holy Toledo, Sally. I'm glad you're safe. Come on in the living room, we've drawn the blinds. Where have you been? You had us all worried. Are you feeling all right? Do you want something to eat?"

Sally suddenly realized she was famished but couldn't face the fuss of a special meal. "A glass of milk, if you please, Walter," she said. Since they were passing through the kitchen, Walter opened the refrigerator, exclaiming, "Dear me, are you sure that's all you want? Oh, my, you've given us a time, Sally! Nobody's been able to sleep for worry. The police aren't happy about you escaping from their washroom. But all that's in the past. The question is what do we do *now*." He spilled some milk on the table, mopped it up with paper towels.

Sally said, "I didn't escape from a washroom, Walter."

Walter looked goggle-eyed. "You said you were going to the bathroom," he recited to her, as if refreshing a faulty memory. "And after that little

disturbance ended, we waited for you to come
out. Finally, they went in and found you had
slipped away. How did you do it? The police would
like to know. They think you're Mrs. Houdini.''

She sighed. "I'll tell you later, if it's all right
with you.''

He handed her the dripping milk glass. The
realization came to her that Walter was an absent-
minded bumbler around the house, and that Charlotte had to be extra efficient to make up for him.
The thought made her like Charlotte better.
Walter, too, she discovered with surprise.

As they made their way to the living room, he
asked, "Did you hear Pastor John on the radio?''
She said she had. "What'd you think of it? Don't
you think what he said made sense?''

She said, "Well, yes, it's just that I—'' She didn't
finish. The living room was illuminated with the
same dim light. There was no coaster for her milk.
She thought of setting it down on the coffee table
to see how good old efficient Charlotte handled a
milk ring. She placed it on a magazine instead.
Charlotte put her head in, said, "You know where
the john is, Sally,'' and disappeared in the direction of the laundry room.

Walter had thrown off his effusiveness and was
soberly attentive. "You have things to tell me, Sally,'' he said. He sat back and crossed his legs,
gestures intended, she guessed, to put her at ease.

"Mostly things to ask you, Walter,'' she said.
"You *are* my lawyer, aren't you?''

"Of course. Of course.''

"Then I guess I owe you some explanations. I
apologize for leaving you standing there in the

police station with egg on your face. But what would you have done if I had come to you and told you I was going to bust out? Would you have said, 'Go ahead, have a good day'?"

He rubbed his nose. "I honestly don't know what I would've done. Probably try to talk you out of it."

She said, "You see!" She proceeded to present her case for "busting out" more strongly than she had to anyone else in the last two days. He tried to pooh-pooh the idea that the police would consider the case closed with her arrest, but his voice had little conviction. It was obvious that he, too, had believed as the police had that Little Sally had simply gone berserk again. She asked Walter to tell her exactly what happened, starting with the moment when he heard the shotgun blast.

"Glad to," he said in his anxious-to-help voice. "I wasn't sleeping well. I never do after a big party. I knew it was a shotgun, I've heard enough of them, only I wasn't positive it came from your house. So I telephoned and got no answer. Should I go over, or shouldn't I go over? I started back to bed, then I said to myself, it's better to make an idiotic fool of myself than take a chance that one of you is hurt and I'm not there to help. So I put on my bathrobe, got the key and padded over."

She said, "Yes, that's right. I'd forgotten we'd given you a spare key."

"Just as you have ours," he said, "I rang the doorbell, but obviously you didn't hear it."

She frowned, trying to remember. "I didn't know you rang the bell. I think I heard the telephone but not the doorbell, isn't that funny?"

"Then I unlocked the door and went in."

"Are you sure the door was locked? Could it have been unlocked?"

"I don't think so, Sally. I was there several times and it was always locked. Anyway, I went up the stairs, calling 'Anybody home,' feeling like a complete ninny. I went to the bedroom doorway and switched on the light. Well, you saw it, I don't have to tell you what I saw. The gun was on the floor near the door. I didn't see you at first, then I heard you moaning. There you were, flopped in the corner like a rag doll. You were a sight. Some blood had spattered on you. You don't want me to go into what happened after that, do you?"

"No, that's enough," she said, reliving the awful, interminable moments when she had cringed in the corner of the bedroom.

The blood was roaring in her ears as it had that night. She was trying to train her ears' memory on the elusive sequence of sounds. "You mentioned hearing," she said slowly. "You told me what you saw, but not what you heard. Sounds, Walter, please. What else did you *hear* besides the shot and my moaning?"

"Gee, Sally, I wasn't paying attention." The pale pink face knotted in concentration. "I heard the shot. I was sitting up in bed, shocked. There were no other noises, maybe a car starting up. Possibly I imagined it. You know how it is when you're straining to hear in dead silence. I think I heard a car, but it didn't register completely because it sounded familiar, like it belonged to someone on the block.

"Very well. I heard myself moving around, I

heard myself on the telephone, et cetera, I heard all the noises I made, the doorbell, the key in the lock, me calling out, the squeaky steps of the staircase—it's funny how loud they can sound in the middle of the night and you don't even hear them in the daytime— then me pushing the bedroom door open, it was partly open, and then clicking on the light.''

Sally was once again listening through the roar. The movement at the doorway, that was the killer going through, pulling the door half shut. Did she hear the squeaky steps? Yes. Yes, because the killer was hastening, hitting the treads hard. Now Sally was backing away from the horror on the bed, past the open window, the rushing sound in her ears. . . she did hear something from outdoors. An engine starting, rattling, purring. ''Did the car have a rattling sound for a few seconds before it went smoothly?'' she asked.

''I'm not even sure I heard it,'' he said with a hint of exasperation. ''It just sounded like I heard it before, and it was not out of place.'' He reordered his features to show the patience and concern of the Walter Keller everybody loved.

She said, in a wavering voice, ''I think I just crossed you off my list of suspects, Walter.''

''Oh? I didn't know you had one.''

''It isn't a very exclusive list. Practically everyone in Savage Point is on it. Steve's mother believes the whole community killed him.''

''I know. I talked to her.''

''Were you the red-headed boy in the launch?''

He looked genuinely puzzled. ''I don't get you,'' he said.

"When you were a high-school kid, did you run the launch for the Savage Point fleet?"

He shook his head as if to clear it, uncrossed his legs, tried to smile. She studied his snub-nosed face in the silence that pulsated to the disco beat from upstairs. "Holy cow, suddenly we're way back on memory lane," he said. "Yes. I drove the launch for, I think, three years. How'd we get way back there from here?"

She watched the expressions that flickered across his face. "You're remembering, aren't you? You're remembering Betty Cochran and Cotton Savage."

He put a fist on his head and stared downward, mouth agape, with the idiotic look of bafflement. "Wait," he said. "Was that her name? If she's the one I'm thinking of. . . . I don't think she meant to do it, she was just so lively and so, what'll I say, so nicely packaged that she roused the beast in an adolescent boy."

"A middle-aged man, too."

"Gee whiz, it was just one summer and I'd long ago forgotten her name, but now that you mention it. . . . Are you sure it was Betty Cochran?"

"Steve's mother."

"Steve's mother!" He was looking at her in shocked disbelief, the fist still on his head as though to keep it from exploding. "So that's it," he said. "I knew something funny was going on. Steve's mother! I never knew. Boomer was trying to tell me something. When I told him you two were moving in next door, he wanted me to call it off. It's not a good idea, he said, for partners to live next door to each other. But you'd already signed the papers. So that's what he was trying to tell me, and couldn't." A look of puzzlement chased the others from his face. "But what? I still don't get it. That Steve's mother lived here thirty years ago? What's so important about that?"

"Think back," she said. "What did Betty Cochran do when your launch took her to her boat?"

"How do I know? She sailed it." His little eyes brightened. "No, she didn't. I don't remember her ever sailing it. She swam. She went way out there to swim, instead of at the dock. I thought that was funny. She did a lot of swimming between her boat and the *Lord Jim*. Yeah... I remember thinking—I thought I saw the— Well, I had a nasty imagination, and I thought all sorts of things." He was red-faced with embarrassment. "You know how boys are," he said. He looked at her quizzically. "You're saying that Steve's mother and Cotton Savage had an affair?"

"I'm saying that Cotton Savage is Steve's father."

He shook his head as if dazed, laughed nervously. "And Boomer knew about this," he said. "He must have. He has a great loyalty to Cotton Savage. Some people think of him as a loudmouth, but he's awfully close-mouthed about Savage family secrets. He and I are close, but he never breathed a word of this. Not even to me." He paused. "And I'm responsible for bringing you and Steve to Savage Point. Can you ever forgive me?"

She said she forgave him—with an unspoken reservation. She never could tell when a lawyer was telling the truth or shading it in order to win a point. Her mind, trying to find reason, leaped a

moment later to Cotton's stroke. "Don't you see,"
she said, "that Steve's conception on the *Lord Jim*
has to have a bearing on his death. But how, that's
the question. Why did someone feel it was necessary to kill him? Was it a vendetta, an evening of
old scores? I think the answer is hidden in the
Savage family history. That's why you have to tell
me about the old man's stroke, Walter."

He frowned, cleared his throat, moved his shoulders as though putting on his barrister's robe. "I
think you're about to put me in a peculiar spot.
You're going to ask a lawyer to give confidential
information about one client to another client. If
you think the Savages had anything to do with
Steve's death, then I have to wonder if I'm in a
conflict-of-interest situation."

Sally said, "Look at it this way. Since Steve was
a Savage, too, and I'm his wife, then we are all one
family—and all one client." Seeing his frown
deepen, she said, "I'm not asking for confidential
information. I simply want you, as my lawyer, to
help me find out who killed my husband. Help me,
Walter."

His ethical problem seemingly resolved, he
donned his reassuring smile. "I'll do what I can,"
he said. "About the stroke, what can I say? He had
it, and it crippled him. And he's been that way
ever since."

"That was ten years ago."

"Just about."

"And the family wanted you to go into court and
have him declared incompetent. Was the whole
fortune in his name?"

"You're getting close to the line," he warned

her, "but since you're a member of the family, I guess I can answer. Yes, everything was in his name. Still is."

"Isn't that bad estate planning? Won't the government take most of it when he dies?"

He sighed. "He's a pigheaded man, Sally, and a suspicious one. When I raised the question of distributing it bit by bit and putting the rest of it in trust, he began to look at me with suspicion. I think he suspected I was in a conspiracy with the family against him. So I dropped it."

"Was Boomer Smith part of the conspiracy?" she asked. Walter Keller sighed loudly. She said, "I mean, was the whole family in on the plot to have him declared incompetent, and was Boomer a part of it?"

"I'm not going to answer that," he said too loudly. "There was no plot! Cotton had trouble with his speech, he was crippled, and there was a possibility, more than a possibility, that his mind was impaired. They came to me with Boomer and we talked about it. It was I who called in the neurologist. When the specialist declared that Cotton's reasoning powers were not affected, everybody accepted it, and that was the end of it. There was no plot!"

"How did Cotton Savage take it?"

"How do I know how he took it?" Walter Keller almost shouted. "We never said anything in front of him! He didn't know what we were thinking!"

Sally let the matter drop, believing the smart lawyer had given himself away. He was as much a part of the plot as the others, and old Cotton must have known about it . . . explaining Walter's nervousness regarding the old man. She asked, "Who does he leave his money to in the will?"

Walter looked pained. "You know I can't tell you that."

She put on a patently false smile. "Does he leave anything to me, his loyal and loving daughter-in-law?"

Walter laughed. "All right, you win. But I'll only tell you this. There's nothing particularly unusual about the will. Some bequests to them all, a life estate for his sister, remainder to the rest. And that's all I'll say about it. Period. My lips are sealed. And don't ever tell anybody I told you that much."

"No mention of Steve?"

Walter had his hands over his mouth to indicate sealed lips. He simply shook his head in answer to her question. Then he let out a snort, and put his hands down. "You said I was on your list of suspects," he said. "Did you really, honestly think I belonged there? I'm hurt that you—"

"Walter, you had the key," she explained. "The killer had to have a key to get in. You were the only one I knew who had a key. I'd forgotten it until you mentioned it. That's when you went to the top of the list."

"Then why'd you cross me off?" he asked. Suddenly he held up his hand. "Hey, wait a minute, I just changed my mind. If the Savages and Boomer Smith are on it, I'd like to be on it, too."

"Sorry, you're definitely off—until I find out something that'll make me put you back on. You're off because I believe it was the killer we heard driving off in a car. Since you lived next door, it doesn't stand to reason that you'd *drive* from the scene of the crime. You'd walk."

The doorbell suddenly sent shrieks through Sally's nerves. She jumped up and started toward the rear door. Walter's voice stopped her. "Whoa, don't run. It's probably only Virginia." Seeing her look, he explained, "I called her when you first arrived. I thought she could help." As he went to the door, he muttered, "Now I'm not so sure."

Sally stopped, held rigid by outrage. She had trusted Walter Keller and he had betrayed her. From all she had learned, the Savage family was her enemy, and now Walter was delivering her into the hands of one of them. Somebody wanted her to be caught by the police to cover Steve's murder. Would Virginia be alone, or would she have the police with her? Frantically, Sally considered her options: to dash out the back door into the arms of the waiting watcher, or face the less certain perils represented by Virginia Goldsboro. She stayed where she was. After all, Virginia was an ecologist, and ecologists don't destroy life, they preserve it, don't they?

Virginia strode in, spouting big rocks of sentences in a volcano of words. "You said you had a visitor, Walter, but you didn't say who it was! This *is* a surprise. Is she all right? Ah, Sally!" She beamed down at Sally, who was holding her breath. "Oh, no, you can't be frightened of me! You poor dear, I'm sure you've been through hell, and I can't blame you. But I'm here as a *friend*, I don't care whether you did this awful thing or not. I mean to say I'm sure you *didn't* do it. It's not *in*

ore

you to do something like that. Here, sit down. Is
that all Walter gave you? Milk? Who do you think
did this crazy thing? What can we do to help?''

Virginia was standing over her. Before Sally
could think of anything to say, Virginia said, ''Let
me say one thing that I think'll help, and then I'll
hold my peace. I'll say it once, and shut up. I think
you should go to the police and let them handle
whatever it is you think you're doing. They're
only after the truth, the same as you. There, I've
said it.'' She moved away and plopped into a
chair.

Sally glared at Walter Keller who, in his distress,
looked like he was about to cry. ''Honest, I was
thinking of you,'' he said. ''I thought Virginia
could help. I still do.... Tell her what you learned
from Steve's mother. Whatever else, Virginia will
be honest with you, I guarantee it.''

Sally turned her cold stare on Virginia. ''Did you
bring the police with you?''

Virginia laughed. ''Heavens, no. I didn't have to.
They're right next door.'' Sally wouldn't have
noticed the squint lines if she weren't looking for
them; they were there, the result of surrounding
muscles straining to help nearsighted eyes see better. Aside from these marks of vanity, Sally could
see nothing but candor in the face, in the square
jaw, the thin, smiling lips, the blue eyes themselves.

Confusion replaced Sally's bristling animosity.
''Are you going to call them?'' she asked sullenly.

''Not I,'' Virginia said. ''I was hoping you
would.''

Sally asked, ''Do you know who Steve was?''

Virginia nodded. "I think so. But *you* tell *me*."

Sally tried to unclench her fists and couldn't. "When did you find out that Steve was your Uncle Cotton's son?" she asked.

"I began to suspect it before the closing," Virginia said in a conversational tone. "I knew about Betty Cochran, of course, from way back, but it's a common name, and when Walter brings in a partner named Cochran thirty years later, who's to suspect the connection? Gradually, it struck me that something in his looks, his voice, was familiar. I didn't know for sure until Saturday night...here. But," she added, "I don't know who killed him, I'm sorry."

Sally said, "I know it was somebody connected with the Savage family."

"You *know*?" Walter said.

"Well, I'm pretty sure. It's the only connection. Walter, where does an illegitimate child stand in the law? In regard to inheritance, I mean."

"Nowhere, if the estate is disposed of by will."

"Could Steve have stood to inherit something?"

"No way, under the circumstances." Walter's voice was emphatic.

"Was Mr. Savage planning to change his will, maybe to include Steve?"

Walter shook his head, and replied in his magisterial voice. "Sally sweetheart, Cotton has known of the child in Mamaroneck for thirty years. He didn't put him in the will I drew for him twelve years ago, and there is no reason for him to include him now. On the contrary, if I know Mr. Savage, he wouldn't for a moment consider broadcasting an ancient indiscretion by naming an il-

legitimate son in his will. No, I can almost say for
sure he wasn't planning to change his will."

Virginia said softly, "I think we'd have known if
he were."

"There're no secrets in the family, are there?"
Sally said bitterly. "Since the existence of the boy
growing up in Mamaroneck was personally known
only to Betty Cochran and Cotton Savage, how'd
you and the rest of the family find out about him?
I don't imagine Cotton told you."

"No, he didn't. It was none of our damned business!" An acidity edged into Virginia's voice.
"That's the way dear Uncle Cotton felt about it.
But even a man like him can't hide checks in the
amount of four hundred dollars a month for the
past thirty years. It doesn't sound like much, but
do you know what it's added up to? A hundred
and forty-four thousand dollars! To me, that's a lot
of bread... and a lot of crust."

"You resented it," Sally said.

"Of course!" Virginia said. "If he's going to give
away money like that—and it's uncharacteristic,
believe me—he should do it *in* the family, not outside. Charity begins at home, and some of us could
be listed among the hundred neediest cases." She
laughed. "But I'm dramatizing, naturally. We're
not exactly undernourished."

"You say you knew about the money going to
Betty Cochran, but how'd you know about the
child? Steve's mother swears no one knew about
it."

Virginia replied evenly, "Aunt Edith knew
about it before she died, and she must've told my
mother and Boomer Smith, or let it slip somehow.

Anyhow, I overheard mother and Boomer talking about it. I was only a teenager, but I had one big set of ears." She laughed.

Sally was trying to retain a hold on reason. "But how would Edith have known?" she said. "She was the wronged wife. Are you saying that her husband actually told her?"

Virginia shrugged. "I don't know every detail, Sally, and I don't think it's very important today. What I *have* believed through the years, because my mother told me, is that Uncle Cotton confessed to Edith that he was in love with that woman and asked for a divorce. It wasn't hard for Edith to deduce that they had slept together. But I doubt very much that he told her about the child. I don't know how she found out about it."

"I know," Walter said, quite unexpectedly. The two women stared at him. "That is, I think I know," he amended. "But I shouldn't say anything without Virginia's consent."

"Go ahead," Virginia said. "Tonight our family history is an open book. Let's not hold anything back."

"Well, it's only what Boomer told me last night," Walter said, on the defensive. "On the day that the love child, as they say, was born, months later in Mamaroneck, the aggrieved wife of the man got a telephone call from the aggrieved husband of the woman. Mike Cochran said to Edith Savage something to the effect, 'You don't know me, but the child of your husband was just born to my wife in Mamaroneck, I can't stand it and I'm leaving. I advise you to do the same.' Anyway, that's Boomer's story."

"Boomer's got a big mouth," Virginia said.

"Oh, on the contrary," Walter said quickly. "I've been a close friend of his since I was a boy, and he's never violated a confidence that I know of. Last night, when he had his little run-in with Sally, he came here and he needed a drink. That was a surprise, because as you know he smokes like a fiend, but he drinks very little. Because of Tish, I believe. He'd just had his encounter with Sally, and he was upset. That's when he told me all this."

Something was out of kilter with the story, Sally thought. She said, "The picture I get of Edith is that she was a proud and prudish woman. I just can't see her telling something like that to her doctor, especially a young doctor."

Virginia gave her a mystified look.

Walter said, "Let me try to be precise. Boomer didn't say she *told* him, if it makes any difference, just that was the story he got from her."

Virginia said, "Spoken like a weaseling attorney, Walter."

"An uplifting note to end on," Walter said briskly. "But let's get back to Sally's present predicament. The both of us think she should go to the police. But it's not our decision to make. It's hers."

"Not so fast, Walter," Sally said, moving to the edge of her chair. "Just a few minutes ago, you seemed surprised, to say the least, when I told you Steve was Cotton's son. That was a great job of acting, wasn't it?"

Walter flushed, hung his head. "I didn't know a blessed thing until I talked with Boomer last night, that's the truth. And I wasn't really positive it was Steve we were talking about until you told me. Well, maybe I did act a little bit. I had to find out how much you knew, and I was playing it by ear."

"One other thing, Mr. Actor. Our key, the key to our house—where did you keep it?"

"On one of the key hooks in the kitchen. You know the plywood thing Henry carved in school."

"By the back door?"

"Right."

"In open view?"

"Yeah. Why?"

"Oh, Walter!" she exploded. "Anybody in Savage Point could've gotten his hands on it in the past three months. It had a tag on it, right? And the tag said, 'Cochran,' right? Well, hell's bells, now we have no way of knowing who might have duplicated the key. Unless you have a handy list of residents who passed through your kitchen between June and September."

Walter bridled. "I know you're under terrible strain, Sally, but I don't think that little outburst was called for. We took as good care of your key as we do of our own. Did you expect us to keep it in a safe-deposit box?"

"I'm sorry, Walter," Sally said, "but I'm so frustrated! It's possible someone lifted the key, had a copy made and then put it back. How many people *did* parade through your kitchen this summer?"

Walter gave her a helpless look. "Just about everybody in Savage Point, I'm afraid."

"Did anybody notice it missing at any time?"

He sighed. "It's the sort of thing nobody'd

notice. You were here Saturday night. Did you
look?''

"No, I didn't, but that's different,'' she said. It
wasn't different, and she knew it. Suddenly she
felt claustrophobic, though the Keller living room
was large. Her chair was an enveloping one, but
what was really closing in on her were all the tantalizing facts she had learned...and the big zeros
they added up to. Uttering a low growl, she did a
back flip toward the entrance hall; then, pounding
the air with her arms, she jumped up and down as
if smashing her sense of hopelessness underfoot.
Then, her voice rising to a keen, she dove into a
handstand, sprang madly up and down on her
hands...until she lost her balance and fell into
the entrance hall, where she lay, laughing and crying uncontrollably. Walter Keller was standing
over her, Virginia beside him, Charlotte at the dining room arch, Sneaky Henry and his pudgy
brother and sister on the stair landing.

Sally said, "You should see yourselves from
down here. My, what big nostrils you have! I think
I'll lie here for a moment.'' She knew she had done
the worst thing possible—she had acted like an insane person, practically foaming at the mouth.
The heaving in her chest slowed, and she said,
"Gee, that felt good. It's a variation on the primal
scream bit. You all should try it sometime.'' She
jumped to her feet, and the others recoiled at the
unexpected move.

"I'm sorry, people," she said. "What you have
just seen was a tantrum, nothing more. You won't
believe this, but it actually proves I'm sane, not insane." To the kids on the stairs, she said, "The

show is over. Time for a commercial." When they
didn't move, she said, "That's all there is, there
ain't no more. Honest."

Charlotte looked up at them, said, "Scat," and
they disappeared. She put her arm around Sally's
shoulder and guided her back to the living room.
"Obviously your nerves are in a sorry state,
neighbor. What you need is a good night's sleep.
Sit down for a while and compose yourself.
Walter, don't you think you ought to check
whether the police heard the rumpus? Virginia, do
you suppose you could put her up for the night? I
don't think Walter can risk putting her up here."

Sally said, "I don't want to sit."

Virginia said, "We'd be delighted to bed her
down at Greystone, Charlotte. It'd give me a
chance to get to know my cousin-in-law better.
The poor dear's been through a harrowing time."

"Hey, I'm here. Talk to me," Sally said.

Virginia impulsively put her arm around Sally's
shoulder, wrestling her away from Charlotte. "I'm
sorry, Cousin Sally," she said, squeezing her.
"Your tantrum, as you call it, kind of knocked the
brains out of my head. Please, we very much want
you to stay overnight, or as long as you want, at
Greystone. There're no police there. It's the least
we can do, since it seems that Steve has suffered
much, if your theory is correct, at the hands of the
Savage family. We all want to shelter our new
cousin."

Sally pulled away. "That's very gracious, Cousin
Virginia," she said, lapsing into her childhood accents, "but I declare Cousin Charles might not
agree. I get the distinct impression he's trying to

bury me in the booby hatch. Don't you get that impression, too, Cousin Virginia?''

"Cousin Charles is a nincompoop. He never should've spoken to the police. Believe me, I gave him a thorough bawling out. The jackass thought he was doing his civic duty.''

"By lying about me?''

"Come, Cousin Sally, he was only reporting what he thought he saw and heard. Obviously, he was mistaken.''

"But, dear Cousin Virginia, I've been made to understand that the people of Savage Point do not get involved. Yet Cousin Charles voluntarily went to the police station and relayed his mistaken information to them.''

Virginia said, "I am not my cousin's keeper.''

"I've been made to understand that you were.''

Virginia said, "Why are you picking a fight with me? You must also have been made to understand that Cousin Charles is not the brightest person in the world. I love him dearly, but the fact is, he's a dim bulb. Now, are you coming or not?''

Sally said, "Yes.''

Virginia said with surprise, "You are?''

"Yes, and I'm very grateful to you," Sally said. "The reason I came here was to beg Walter to take me to see Mr. James Cotton Savage because he is the key figure in my husband's murder.''

"You're crazy—I mean, you can't be right.''

Sally said, "Oh, I don't think the old man even knew anything about it. To me, this whole thing is a puzzle and he's the missing piece. So don't be mad at me. I'm excited at finally getting to talk to my husband's father. Let's go now.''

Virginia said, "Hold on a minute. There's no way you'll be able to see him tonight. He goes beddy-bye right after the children's hour. He's sacked in for the night. Tomorrow is another story. You'll get a chance to talk to him then for a little while."

Sally felt her sense of frustration returning and was barely able to push it back. It was clear to her that the gentlefolk of Savage Point were in a conspiracy to prevent her from getting to James Cotton Savage.

She said, "That'll be fine, then. I'll come tomorrow."

Walter, who had strolled to the front porch as if checking the weather and had returned with an all-clear shake of his head, interrupted. "But where are you going to stay tonight? It's turning nasty out there."

Charlotte Keller, who had stayed in the background, started to say, "Really you shouldn't, Sally—"

Sally said, "It's all right, Char. I'll be in a warm, comfortable place." In fact, she had no idea where she would stay; she hadn't thought that far ahead. She added, "The same place I stayed last night," knowing she shouldn't go back to the DiGiorgios' boat.

Charlotte said, with real concern in her voice, "Can you tell us where that is? No, I don't suppose you can. I really think you should go to the police, but I imagine you've already said no to that."

Walter said, "Dear me, Sally, you could be shot before you even get there."

Sally said, "I've done a pretty good job of staying out of their sight so far—"

"Sure, by climbing along the seawall," Virginia said.

Sally was losing control again. She said, "It's safer than walking the streets. For me, anyhow. It'd take an *army* of cops to keep me from getting around the point, if I wanted to." She clamped her jaws shut to cut off this childish bravado.

Virginia said, "Very well, Sally, have it your way. I'm sorry we didn't hit it off better. Maybe we will tomorrow. Is eleven o'clock convenient for you?"

Sally suddenly felt ashamed of herself. This big, likable woman had come in answer to a call for help, and Sally had done nothing but heap abuse on her. And the woman had taken it with heroic forebearance. Sally gave her a quick kiss on the cheek. "Eleven is fine," she said. "And I hope we hit it off better tomorrow. Thank you very much for coming." She felt the tears starting to come, and turned away.

Virginia said, "My pleasure." She said goodbye to the Kellers and left.

Walter turned back from the door with glistening eyes. "That woman is a peach," he said. To Sally, he said, "You really should've gone, you know."

Sally said she knew.

"I'm worried about you," he said.

"I know," she said.

"So, client to lawyer, where are you staying?"

"I can't tell you."

"You don't trust your lawyer?"

"It isn't that."

"I understand," Walter said with a pained

expression. "You don't trust anybody. Tell me this much. Do you have far to go?"

"Not far," she said. Actually, the only place she could think of was Barney Harper's, which wasn't a safe place for her at all, but the only place.

"Then I'm going to insist that my son escort you part of the way."

"I won't hear of it." She didn't even know in which direction she would go after leaving the house.

"Just part of the way," Walter insisted. "I don't want to pry your secret hiding place out of you, or find out who's sheltering you. I just wouldn't feel I'd done my part if I let you go out of here alone."

Her nerves were tightening up again; she couldn't stand another minute of Walter's wheedling. So she agreed to an escort by Sneaky Henry, determined to ditch him at the first opportunity. When Henry came down the stairs with a smirk on his face, she knew she'd made a mistake. All she said to him, however, was, "Let's go, Mr. Escort."

Walter was fluttering nervously once again, asking did she have everything, was there anything she needed. Charlotte gave her a plastic-wrapped sandwich. Walter gave her a quick hug, then clicked off the living room light. In the darkness, Sally and Henry slipped out the back door, turned right, away from the Cochran house.

"Stay close," she whispered to Henry, who was behind her. He put his hand on her rear end. "Not that close," she hissed. The hand retreated. Her initial plan was to circle around her house, give it a wide berth, then head back across the spine of Savage Point to Harper's Cove, groping her way

from backyard to backyard, parallel to Dover
Road. In the first backyard, next door to the
Kellers, she cracked her shin on a wheelbarrow. In
the second backyard, Henry snagged his sweater
on a tree branch. She realized her plan was hopeless: the backyards at night were *terra incognita*
bristling with unknown dangers, fences, bikes,
rakes, wading pools, German Shepherds and angry
owners. Moreover, since it was a direct route to
Barney's, she'd be giving Henry a pointer to
where she was going. Her only alternative was
to go by way of the seawall, after all. "Sorry," she
whispered to Henry; "just a few more."

They crossed Dover Road just east of the Cotton
Estates, and started the torturous journey through
the backyards bordering the marsh of Little Neck
Bay. Henry helped her over fences by placing a
hand on her backside. When she made him go first,
he was there to catch her by accidentally clutch-
ing her breast and holding her until he was sure
she was steady. She knew ways of protecting
herself that would be surprising and painful to
him, but someone else's backyard was not the
place to execute them. She decided to bear with
him until they got to the seawall, where she could
easily outsprint him. Meanwhile, the only harm he
was doing was slowing her progress. He whispered, "Oops" every time his hand "slipped."

The backyards ended where Shore Road swung
to the shoreline, not far from her first hiding place
that she had quirkily dubbed the Sally S. Cochran
Memorial Duck Blind. Between here and the dock
there was scant cover; they made their way along
the waterline, over boulders, through marshy

patches. Henry's hands were constantly on her, as if solicitous of her balance, but the need to watch her footing and be on the alert for possible observers on the road above them, as well as her urgent desire to get to the seawall and away from the boy, made her ignore the insulting hands.

They paused at the dock to study its emptiness. Henry's hands were busily "helping" her. "I'm going to tell your father, you know," she whispered. He whispered, "Ah, be a good sport." She glared at him in the semidarkness. He whispered, "Anyway, who'd believe you?" An elbow in the ribs removed the hands. "You didn't have to do that," he said.

Three kids were drinking beer and smoking pot in the shelter of the hedge bordering the road. Sally and Henry scampered in a crouched position below the seawall, made their way under the dock, across the little beach and over the rock jetty to the seawall beyond. Henry slipped on a wet rock and hurt his ribs. He sat on the seawall and groaned softly. She could easily have walked away from him but didn't. She bent over him, soothing him, fearing that something was broken. He gripped her shoulder, pulled himself erect, accidentally touching her breast. "Oops," he said. She sighed.

Being the quarry, she was starting to think like a fox. She decided to leave a false scent by giving him a misleading hint of where she was heading. Remembering the Silverman house was near the point, she said, "You're incorrigible, Henry. I should've taken a taxi to Maxie's, instead."

He said, "What?"

She said, "Never mind." If the hint were passed on, Sam and Maxine would be given an uncomfortable few minutes by the police, and that was all.

This stretch of the seawall was adequately shielded by stunted pine. They made their way along the top, Sally in the lead, ignoring the hand, looking for the best spot to start her goodbye sprint. Not here, at the foot of the Greystone property, where the wall had treacherous areas of stone rubble. Not the next section, either, where it curved and was partially blocked by shrubs. The next straightaway would be it, she decided.

She sensed, rather than saw or heard, someone on the seawall ahead of them. Signaling Henry to silence, she led him by the hand back to the crumbling stone stairs leading down to the boulders at the base of the wall. They waited, but no one came. She signaled for him to follow her over the boulders close to the wall. The going was difficult. Each footstep had to be tested for safety before the next one was taken; it had to be done in silence. Henry, who had fallen once, was picking his way carefully. He hadn't touched her for ten minutes. Thank God for small favors, she thought. They came to a small strand of beach between boulders, and rested a moment.

She should have expected it but didn't. Suddenly Henry had her pinned against the seawall, his heavier body against hers, his hand roughly trying to push down inside her jeans. That does it, she thought; this is where the obscene boy and I part company, for better or worse. She struggled to arrest the hand while pondering the best way to push him off, hesitating only because she didn't want to crack his skull on the surrounding rocks. The eeriness of the silence in which they tussled— with a measure of desperation on her side as well as his, for he was the stronger—was not lost on her. Someday she might see the humor of it, but at the moment the mute embrace in the unsheltering darkness at the foot of the rough seawall, which at this point reared to a height of twelve feet, dwarfing them, was quite humorless.

Someone called her name.

No, it wasn't a call, it didn't shatter the silence or break the darkness; rather, it insinuated itself and became part of the air surrounding her. "Sally?" Not a voice but a questioning whisper that, if spoken on stage, would have carried to the last seat in the darkened gallery. Hoarse, sexless. So unexpected was it and so startled was she that she responded automatically, "Yes?" aloud. She wondered if she imagined it. It had come out of the darkness high above her, beyond the lip of the seawall against which she was pinned. She looked up, saw the black wall against the empty gray sky; no one there but the tips of peeping tree branches. Her grip on Henry's intruding arm relaxed, and the groping hand slid downward. Scarcely two seconds after she had cried, "Yes," another automatic response brought her two arms up and out and her knee up and into the groin, sending the ardent youth reeling away from her.

In the same instant she heard heavy steps atop the wall, a grunt and an indrawn breath, a woman's gasp. What happened next she saw in a series of stop-action shots. Something, a projectile, at first shapeless and then quite sharply defined, left the seawall and flew through the air, at first in a jackknifed position, then splayed, so that the soaring woman—clearly, she wore a dress—was silhouetted against the distant sky, arms flapping witlessly as if trying to fly or swim, the legs trailing like twin tails on a kite, the dress lazily changing shape in the air. No sound. In Sally's mind, the figure hung suspended for long seconds. She couldn't make out the face. Then it plummeted and smashed into the boulders with a scarcely audible whomp, even as Henry came heavily to rest five yards away. The body settled and was still.

Nothing moved but the water and wind. She was rigid against the stone wall, Henry momentarily shocked into immobility, his imploded breath trapped in his lungs. The silence was accentuated by the distant drone of motors on the Cross Island and in the low approaches to LaGuardia.

"Sally?" This time the hoarse whisper was directly above her, but Sally could see nothing but the wall and the cloud-shrouded sky. Henry's pent-up breath burst from him in a wail that commenced in the high registers, descended, trailed off. It could have been mistaken for a woman's scream. In the ensuing silence, Sally thought she heard the scrape of stone fragments, the barest suggestion of footsteps. She pressed against the wall, thoroughly frightened and yet outraged. Henry was moving, groaning. No further sound from above. Henry sat leaning against a boulder, one hand at his crotch, the other at his rib cage. She felt no sympathy for him. Carefully, she approached the rag bundle that had hurtled from the sky. Bare legs, loafers, blue dress, sweater, the back of a head. Even before she touched the shoulder to turn it over, she knew who it was. The pale face of Tish Smith was lopsided, one side of it pocked, hieroglyphed, from the rough stone, strangely bloodless. Boomer's unhappy wife was beyond consolation. She was dead. For a moment the bloody mess of Steve's face was there, and she shoved it aside. "No!" she said.

Sally marveled at her own self-control. If ever there was a time for a crack-up, this was it. In the distant reaches of her mind the notion that perhaps at long last she was tough enough to survive loitered, waiting to be brought forward and examined with awe at a later time. Right now the sense of continuing danger commanded her actions. She knew as a certainty that the police would be converging on this spot in a matter of minutes.

Henry, still in a sitting position, had swiveled around and was glaring at her as she crouched over the untidy bag of a body; he was incoherently cursing her. The dead woman's eyes were open in the innocent stare of a child, revealing so much the true essence of the sweet woman that Sally felt she was trespassing. She hid the naked face with Joey's soiled handkerchief.

"You're a sad sack, Henry," she said aloud, too hurried to whisper. "I'm leaving you now, and I don't care what you tell the police." She started away from him over the boulders, jumping recklessly; there was no time to test them for safety. After a short distance, realizing that her progress was slow and that she would sooner or later break a leg at a place where the boulders were piled high against the wall she leaped, grabbed the top of the wall and, half expecting her fingers to be stomped on, awkwardly swung her knee up and over, and scrambled to her feet. She was alone, sheltered by a few scrawny trees.

No time for stealth. She had to make an open run for it, and pray for her guardian angel to cover her presence with a dusty cloud or something...to hide her not only from the police but from the killer. Without pausing to think it through, she knew beyond a shadow of doubt that Tish Smith did not fall accidentally from the seawall, nor did she jump. She was pushed, hurled, impelled by a killer who thought he was dispatching, not Tish Smith, but Sally Cochran to her death.

11:05. BARNEY HARPER'S PLACE was in darkness. She watched it for five minutes, motionless, then stole forward until she was beneath the window of his bedroom. She thought she heard breathing, found it to be the pulse in her own ears. She couldn't tell if Barney was alone in his bachelor's bed or comforting an afflicted housewife in one of his intimate one-on-one sessions. She had no alternative but to chance it.

She tapped lightly on the window and instantly he was there, an indistinct outline in the darkness. She held her face up so he could see it. He said, "Go to the door." It took him longer than she expected for him to get there. No light went on. In darkness, he opened the office door, took her by the shoulder and guided her to the bedroom and closed the door. He sat her on the bed, himself

beside her, his arm still around her shoulder in a
steadying embrace. In the dim light from the windows, she noticed he wore work pants and an unbuttoned work shirt over his bare chest. Dully, she
figured he had slipped them on before coming to
the door.

She said, "I'm sorry, Barney. I had no place to
go."

He said, "I think we'd better not put on a light,
if it's all right with you." He sounded out of
breath. Strange. A person roused from sleep
would not be expected to be breathing laborious-
ly. Unless the person had only just gotten into bed
after a long run.

She said, "Were you there?"

"Where?"

"On the seawall."

"Something happened on the seawall?"

"Yes. Were you there? Was it you?" Suddenly
another image again superimposed itself on Tish's
staring face—the bloody mask of Steve in the bed
beside her. Involuntarily she wiped her hand on
her blue jeans, wiped hard, wiping the remembered blood from it. Had she walked trustingly,
childishly, into the warm comforting grip of her
killer? The face next to her, when she turned to it,
seemed to have slanted feline eyes and the wild
hair rose into horns. Or were the eyes just sleep-
swollen? "Was that you in the bedroom?" she
asked, pulling against the encircling arm, feeling
cold and lost and terribly wrong.

He shook her roughly, brought his fist up under
her nose; the eyes, no longer feline, were blazing
in the dark. "I oughta flatten that goddamn nose

on your face," he growled. The fist touched the
nose. "Jesus," he said, "it's cold and wet like a
dog's." He pulled a handkerchief from his pocket,
handed it to her. "Here. Blow."

"I don't want to blow." she said.

"Blow, anyway!" She took the cloth and wiped
her nose. He said, "You make me so goddamn
mad, Sally. To answer your questions, no, it
wasn't me, whatever that means. I wasn't on the
seawall tonight, and I wasn't in your bedroom. If
you've come over here to accuse me of murdering
your tight-assed husband, you can just take your
butt right out of here before I kick it out!" His
voice was harsher than she'd ever heard it, raspy
enough to make her ears bleed.

She said in a small voice, "All you had to do was
say no. I was just asking. No would have been
enough."

He snorted. "Just asking! All right, so you just
asked and I just answered. Is that the end of
that?"

"Why were you breathing hard when I first
came in?"

Suddenly he laughed and hugged her shoulder.
"That's a damn fool question, do you know that?
I'm not exactly a saint, dear cousin, and when an
attractive young woman pulls me out of bed and
comes into my bedroom, and my arm is around
her, I've been known to pant just a little bit,
though I try not to drool. Actually, I wasn't aware
that I was breathing hard."

She shuddered. "I'm beginning to believe I'm
crazy," she said. "I don't know why I lit into you
like that. You're the only one on Savage Point I

don't suspect." Once again she had to exorcize the devilish question. "Tell me honestly," she said, fixing her eyes on his, "am I really crazy?"

He cackled. "A little tetched in the haid," he said. "But on you it looks good. . . . Now maybe you'll tell me what happened."

Her account was disjointed, stumbling, for she was trying to get the details straight in her head. Henry was harassing her at the base of the wall. She heard her name whispered loudly, but, as she now evoked it, it didn't come from directly above her; it came from a little farther back. She answered, and then Tish came hurtling, landing far out on the boulders. Then came the second whisper, this time directly above her. "Sally?" The murderer wanted to find out whether the fall had killed her. When Henry screamed, the killer went away, probably thinking his victim was still alive but immobilized. That was when she knew the police would come, for the killer wanted the police to find her, dead or alive, and close out Steve's murder, as solved. But instead of Little Sally—"

"Oh, not Tish!" Barney said. "Not Tish!" His tone rose. He roughly pushed Sally away, stood up with his back to her. "That poor, sweet old broad," he said in a wavering voice. "She was one of the nicest, gentlest, kindest, *saintliest*—" He turned to Sally. "She was one of the Lord's holy drunkards," he said in a hushed voice. "She never should've come to Savage Point. She didn't belong. She was too weak and vulnerable. So they've finally dropped her on the rocks and cracked her open, like seagulls do the clams." Sally shivered at the image he evoked. "But why her?" he said. "I really don't get it."

"It wasn't her, it was me," Sally said, reminding him that Tish Smith was a small, slender woman about the same size as Sally, and could easily have been mistaken for Sally when silhouetted against the water in the darkness. "And she was wearing a blue dress, like mine," Sally said. When Barney remained silent, she asked, "Were you in love with her?"

His cackle sounded more like his usual self. "With Tish? My God, no, if you mean did I sleep with her. She was too straight a person for that. She just needed someone to talk to, and I was elected. Those vultures over there treated her like an idiot child. They sucked the pride out of her. She needed someone to build her up with a little gin and sympathy, and a little hard breathing to make her feel desirable. As you know, I'm pretty good at heavy breathing." He tried to laugh, but a catch in his throat stopped it. "If you mean did I love her as a person," he said, "I—I guess I did."

"Is Boomer the villain?" she asked. "Is he really a bully?"

"Bully? Yes, sometimes. Villain, no." He was pacing around the little room in the dark. "I guess he loved her as well as he can love anyone. But why do you think he's such a loudmouth? Because the poor bastard is one of the most insecure persons I've ever met. If you get him alone on a boat and there's no one else there he feels he has to impress, he can be a pretty nice guy. Why he's so unsure of himself I wouldn't know. From what I hear, he's a pretty good doctor, but he doesn't think so. He's not the handsomest guy in the world, and he's more blubber than muscle, and from what I understand he's no Errol Flynn in the bedroom, but so what? I could use the same words to describe myself and a million other slobs who don't go around browbeating their wives. It's just that two such insecure people shouldn't have married each other. So where does that leave us? Nowhere." He dropped down to the bed beside her. "Oh, God," he groaned. "Tish."

Sally put her arm around his shoulder to comfort him, not realizing that they had reversed roles. Though she felt utterly exhausted, she dredged up energy enough to tell him what she had learned of the passionate love affair aboard the *Lord Jim*, and to recount her adventures leading up to the episode at the seawall. His astonishment, evidenced by such expressions as, "Well, I'll be a son of a bitch!" buoyed her sufficiently to help her finish the tale.

Other comments from him punctuated her story. On Cotton Savage, "He screwed everyone else in Savage Point, why should Betty Cochran be any different?" On Steve's parentage, "Jesus, the poor bugger sure picked a lulu of a father. No wonder he turned out the way he did. I'm sorry I wasn't nicer to him." On Walter Keller, "He seems to have his pudgy little fingers into everything." And on Virginia Goldsboro, "I told you that, as witches go, she was all right." When Sally confessed she didn't get the name of Bess Cochran's doctor, Barney said, "You can bet your sweet ass it was young Dr. Everett Boomer Smith. He's practically a member of the Savage family. Come to think of it, he *is* a member of the Savage family."

They tried to reason through her findings to see if they indicated the identity of the killer, but it was a desultory, fatigue-laden conversation. "I think you can rule out Walter Keller," Barney said, "because even that pious bastard wouldn't fling a body on top of his own son."

"I don't think we can rule him out completely," she said. "If he thought it was me he was pushing off the wall, he would've believed I was alone and, therefore, that Henry'd left me. I point this out just to keep the record straight. But I agree he probably didn't do it. And he's not a pious bastard."

"Wait," Barney said, holding up his hand. "Hold on a darn moment. You have jumped to a conclusion that may bring you the Olympic record for conclusion jumping. You've been assuming that the same person committed both murders. And that the motive for the two killings was the same, or at least that the second grew out of the first. But what if there's no connection between the two? It's possible you're faced with two killers and not just one. Chew on that for a while."

Sally groaned, and fell back on the bed. Her body ached, her head was a leaden weight swollen with mental junk compacted by her throbbing skull. She yearned for Steve to come and soothe her, to put his arms around her and protect her and make her warm and cozy. A muscle in her leg twitched. Her stomach was cramping. She remembered when Steve first told her he loved her.

The last day of the trial. The jury foreman said, "Not guilty." Her mind turned white and motionless. Steve held her up with an arm around

*her. Now that she was free she had no place to go.
After a long time, Steve guided her out of the
courtroom. They took a taxi to his one-bedroom
apartment on Murray Hill. He showed her the bed
where she would sleep, he showed her the nice,
comfy hide-a-bed sofa where he would sleep. Then
he looked down at his shoes and sort of dug a toe in
the carpet, the way Gary Cooper did in those old
movies, and he looked up and said, "I think I'm in
love with you, Sally Spencer." And Steve Cochran
shyly put his arms around her and kissed her. For
a second her body recoiled, but right away she
knew she was in snug harbor, and she never
wanted to leave those warm, strong, enveloping
arms.*

She was crying softly into Barney Harper's
pillow. Then arms were holding her, protecting
her, and something was keeping the chill from her
back. Her twitching stopped. She discovered her
thumb was in her mouth. She remembered Aunt
Tina saying, "That's for babies, you're too big for
that." I know I'm grown up now, she said in her
drowsing mind, but I think I'll keep it there just
this once. It tasted of dirt. She remembered making mud pies, with pebbles for raisins, and pre-
senting them to Uncle Joe, who would put his
arms around her and pretend to eat the mud pies,
and he said, "Take it easy, Cousin Sally, simmer
down, you're going to sleep now. Sleep." Funny,
Uncle Joe calling her that. She slept.

The warmth was gone, and she was awake. It
took her many seconds to remember where she
was. The voices came from Barney Harper's office. Light seeped under the door, but it was

menacing. She heard Barney exclaim, "Jesus Christ, Boomer, this is a terrible shock. I'm very sorry." Sally sat up, gazed wildly around the room, at the open chest where Barney wanted her to hide, at the small rear window. She felt battered.

Boomer's voice, as it came to her through the door, alternated between a low rumble and a louder than usual, slightly out-of-control roar. "I didn't come for your sympathy, Harper. And don't call me Boomer. I don't like you, and you don't like me, and let's leave it at that. I came to find out something."

"Anything. What?"

"I know my wife always came to you when she was upset." Sally realized that the rise and fall of Boomer's voice resulted from the deep breaths he was taking.

Barney said, "Strictly friends. Nothing more."

"I know that," Boomer roared. "If I thought there was anything else, I'd have blasted your head off long ago. But I know Letitia, the mother of my children, and—and—"

"I never tried," Barney said.

"Bully for you." A few seconds later, Boomer said, "She was with you yesterday, and she's been acting funny ever since. Would you believe she started nagging me to death about my smoking? Well, tonight I blew up at her, and she left the house, saying she was going for a walk. My first question, did she come here tonight?"

"No."

"Were you at the club? Did she meet you at the club?"

"No. I was here all night."

Sally noticed a quaver in Boomer's heavy breathing and wondered if he was asthmatic. Boomer said, "All right, yesterday, or any time recently. Did Tish sound depressed, I mean deeply depressed, not just down in the dumps because she and I may have had words? I'm sure I'm an occasional subject of your conversations."

"She was down in the dumps, as you say. I tried to cheer her up. I kid her until she snaps out of it."

"That's great. But she didn't say anything that would indicate she was suicidal?"

"You think she *jumped* off the wall?"

"I don't know. That's what I'm trying to find out. Did she?"

"No, Dr. Smith, she didn't. And if you really knew Tish, you'd know she'd never kill herself. Long-suffering was her greatest virtue and her greatest fault. She'd rather die than commit suicide."

"You think this is a joking matter?" An ominous rumble.

"I'm sorry, Boomer," Barney said. "Your wife was a very wonderful person. I apologize for the idiotic thing I just said. It just came out. The point is, I don't think she jumped. And neither do you."

"And neither do the police. They're trying to figure out why she was so far from the wall." In the long awkward silence that followed, Sally felt her heart beating faster. "Well," Boomer said with a sigh, "sorry to've bothered you, Harper. I'll be going."

Barney said, "I had another visitor today."

Sally tensed her body to stop the quivering.

"Sally Cochran," Barney said. She moved silently to the little window and looked out, shuddering at the prospect of once again plunging into the filthy water. "She found out all about Steve."

Boomer said, "I know."

"She was wondering who the doctor was who told Betty Cochran she was pregnant."

"So?"

"It was young Doc Smith, wasn't it?" This wasn't idle curiosity; he was trying to help her fill in the blank spaces. She knew it, and yet was fearful for him. If Boomer were part of a plot that included murder, he could be dangerous.

"I suppose it was," Boomer said. "What does it matter?"

Barney said, "She thinks someone on Savage Point killed Steve and tried to pin the blame on her."

"I know. She told me." There was a scraping of chair legs on the floor. "Now look, Harper—"

"Has it occurred to you, doc, what the police are really suggesting? That if sweet Letitia didn't fall and she didn't jump, then someone pushed her."

"It's none of your—"

"And has it occurred to you that Tish Smith and Sally Cochran were about the same shape and size? And that in the darkness on the seawall, the one could've been mistaken for the other?"

Boomer's rumble: "What're you leading up to?"

"Can you imagine anyone wanting to kill your wife?" Barney asked. "Did that sweet woman have an enemy in the world? Hell, no! You know she didn't. I'm saying that someone wanted to kill Sally Cochran and mistook Tish for Sally. Tish was clobbered to death on the rocks by the same person who blasted the face off Steve Cochran." Sally drew in her breath sharply.

"Oh, come off it, Harper," Boomer growled. "If someone pushed Tish off the wall, it could just as well've been Little Sally herself."

"And why would Sally Cochran want to do a thing like that? Was she mad at Tish?"

"She was mad, period. Capable of anything, and strong enough to do it."

Barney said softly, "You don't really believe that, do you, doc?" Sally heard the creak of a chair and pictured Boomer sitting down again. Barney went on, "Even if it was mistaken identity, the fact is that someone deliberately smashed your wife on the rocks, and it sure looks to me like it was the same person who killed Sally's husband. Don't forget Steve Cochran was my cousin, part of my family. I loved him." Sally frowned in the darkness, and shook her fist at the door.

He added, "Just as you loved your wife. We can't let this murdering bastard get away with it. We don't know who it is, but maybe we can find out. Let's pool our information.... Okay? Sally's convinced me this whole mess goes back to the love affair between Cotton Savage and Betty Cochran. Now, you were the doctor who discovered she was pregnant, weren't you?"

"Yes."

"Did you know it was Cotton's child?"

"Not then. Later."

Sally heard a police siren wailing in the distance, probably on Northern Boulevard.

"When did you find out?" Barney asked.

Boomer let out a breath that turned into a moan. "Are you sure this is going to help find Tish's killer?"

"I think so."

"Do you promise not to tell anyone?"

"Only if it's necessary to pin the murderer."

"I still don't like you, Harper, but I never heard anyone say you didn't keep your word. I'm violating a patient-doctor relation, but here goes." Sally edged toward the door, lowered herself into the nearest chair. "It was the following May," he said in a rumbling monotone, so low Sally had to put her ear close to the door to hear it. "Edith Savage was one of my patients. She was going through a long and difficult menopause. Let me just say it was a difficult time for Cotton, too, and let it go at that. May 15, 1950. That was an unforgettable day in my life. Cousin Charles was just a boy at the time—"

Sally jumped to her feet, scraping the chair on the floor, May 15 was Steve's birthday! Thoughts tumbled in her head like clothes in a dryer. What in heaven's name did his birthday have to do with anything? More immediately, did Boomer Smith hear the noise in the bedroom? She stood motionless. But the voice droned on, as if all the senses of the speaker were focused on a terrible happening of thirty years ago.

"I climbed aboard the *Lord Jim*," Boomer was saying, "and went through the salon direct to the bedroom. Cotton was standing beside the bed. Edith was lying on the bed. In her wedding dress. The awful thing was her face. The eyes were wide open. The mouth was fixed in a grimace of agony, a death mask that seemed to be screeching. I managed to close the lids most of the way, but the muscles around the mouth were too rigid for me to move them. Cotton had the note in his hand. I took it from him and read it.

"I could recite it to you word for word, Harper, but I won't. It was a rather incoherent diatribe against Cotton. Then she said she'd gotten a phone call from their ex-neighbor Cochran confirming the suspicion that'd been burning in her for six months. Perhaps she could've lived with the memory of Cotton's infidelity, which was over and done with, but not with the existence, day by day for the rest of her life, of 'this accursed fruit of his adultery.' Those were her words. You'd have to know her background to understand why. Religion can be a destructive thing." Again his sigh became a groan. "Anyway, she said that since his violation of the marriage occurred on the *Lord Jim*, it was fitting that she should depart from the marriage there. It was fitting also, she said, that the instrument of departure should be rat poison. The poor woman was obviously out of her head. She didn't realize she was letting herself in for an agonizing death.

"That's about it, Harper. Before I realized it, young Charles took the note from my hand and read it. We three were the only ones who ever saw it. I burned it in an ashtray in the salon." The voice stopped.

Sally clamped a hand to her mouth to stifle a groan. What a ghastly burden for an innocent baby to be saddled with!

Barney's voice, "And you signed a death certificate saying it was a heart attack."

Boomer sighed. "Would it have served any purpose, would it have done any good at all to stigmatize the poor crazed woman as a suicide? I ask you, Harper. Did I do wrong?"

"I guess you did the right thing," Barney said softly. "It was a case where hypocrisy was the best policy."

"What? Oh. Well—" Again, the scrape of a chair.

Barney said, "So you knew about Steve right from the start."

"I knew he existed. I didn't know his name. Not until this year when Walter Keller spoke of him and mentioned he came from Mamaroneck. Now I've got to go. The police've taken Tish for an autopsy."

"Who else knew about Steve?"

"No one outside of the family. Goodbye, Harper. I can't say that it's been pleasant."

Sally slumped in her chair, confused and emotionally exhausted. She heard Barney close the door behind Boomer, the car door slam, the motor start and the car depart. The light disappeared from under the door, and a moment later Barney bumped into her. "Oh," he said. "So you heard? How's that for a can of worms?" She suspected his cackling laugh was meant to cover embarrassment and perhaps a higher human feeling, sympathy. He put his hand on her shoulder. "Okay, back to bed," he said. Suddenly a bouncing, moving light came through the front window, and the muted sound of crunching gravel. "Shit, he's back,"

Barney growled. He went into the office, was back
a second later. "Into the trunk," he growled. "It's
the cops." He closed the door, leaving her alone in
the darkness. She looked at the trunk and knew
she could never make herself get into it; and her
stomach turned at the prospect of going once
again through the back window into the murky
water. She went to the front window.

The murmur of male voices sifted through the
door. The police car stood outside, apparently
empty. Sally didn't know how long she had slept
or what time it was. Get moving, she said to herself. But where? She had run out of havens. It was
too late to accept Virginia's invitation to Greystone; undoubtedly, the Savage household would
be asleep. Then she remembered the charred hulk
of the burned-out house behind Greystone. Not
exactly perfect, but it would give her a chance to
keep her date with Cotton Savage in the morning.

She heard Barney say, "Oh, you're invited to
search my bedroom anytime you want, gentlemen." Sarcasm touched with anxiety. She found
the hook holding the window screen, unlatched it,
and slithered out, feet first, as the bedroom door
opened. She picked herself up from her hands and
knees, and in a moment she was racing across the
dirt, past the simple dry-dock frames, toward the
encircling trees.

"There she goes!" The shout came from in front
of Barney's office. Not turning to look, she
guessed it was the second policeman in the prowl
car who had returned outside. "Halt!" She was
nearly to the trees; she couldn't stop for Barney's
sake and because she was in a mood of hysterical

euphoria where nothing could touch her. She heard a shot and her heart said, "Fall!" and she fell forward at the last moment, twisting into a forward roll by which she was instantly on her feet and running again. She had heard no bullet zitt past her; it was only a warning shot.

She was in the trees, pummeled by branches, tripped by underbrush, unable to see anything. She ran full force into a chicken-wire fence and was catapulted backward. Dazed, unaware of pain, she followed the fence to where it terminated at the edge of the marsh. She plunged around it, tried to get back on dry land, found she was fenced out, forced to thrash blindly through the reeds, intent on getting away and never mind the noise she was making. She broke out of the reeds onto the primitive, potholed swamp road that connected Savage Point and Little Neck.

She dashed across the road just as an approaching police car caught her in its headlights. "Stop!" She leaped the log railing, slipped into the remaining patch of reeds this side of the railroad tracks. "Sally, stop!" The car had come to a halt on the road behind her; someone was thrashing heavily in her wake. Ahead of her the tracks ran on an elevated embankment across the lowland of Harper's Ravine, steeply pitched and gravel-strewn. Suddenly the embankment just ahead of her glared with the light from the police car's searchlight. She darted to the right along the edge of the embankment, away from the light; she fell and cried out, and her thrashing pursuer yelled, "Over here!" She started her scramble up the sixty-degree pitch while the searchlight wavered,

as if uncertain where "over here" was. Halfway
up, the light found her again, in open view like a
specimen in a display case. "Hold it, Sally!" She
continued to climb upward with hands and feet. A
shot sent gravel sharply against her legs.

Sally wasn't thinking at all. She was panting,
sobbing, following only the animal instinct to run
from danger. A rational person would have
stopped, even while the mind was telling her that
the cops were aiming at her legs, wishing only to
stop her, not to kill her. Her heavy pursuer was
following her up the incline, sliding in the gravel,
receiving in the face the gravel slide loosened by
Sally. She reached the top, nearly clutched the
third rail, grabbed its wooden cover, raised herself
to a half-crouch. Another shot stung her leg.
Scarcely aware she had been hit, she leaped
awkwardly across the tracks, went feet first down
the other side. The cop on the embankment was
shouting, "Go around! Go around! I'll follow her
here!"

When she stopped sliding, she rested with her
back to the embankment, wondering if she would
ever move again. She muttered, "I *am* crazy."
And the one thought her brain, now starting to
function, filtered through to her was, "You crazy
nut, you've now run *away* from Savage Point.
Away from your rendezvous with Cotton Savage.
Gotta get back to the other side of the tracks. Gotta get back." It added, "Of course, you gotta get
away from the cops first."

"Right," she said and moved to her right, away
from the sound of the floundering policeman,
west toward the Savage Point station. The land

rose through an area of trees, and as it did the height of the embankment to her right diminished until it vanished and gave way to an increasingly deep defile through which the tracks ran. She came to an area of fenced backyards, scrambled along below them on the steep wooded slope. After a short distance, she made her way back down to the tracks. "This proves my insanity beyond doubt," she said. "Any sane person would use the whole rest of the country to hide in."

She bounded across the open tracks. Even in the overcast night, she could have been observed along the straight right-of-way from as far away as the Savage Point overpass in one direction and the Little Neck station in the other. It was a risk she had to take. She clambered up the north side of the pass, through trees, and emerged at the bottom of the Piccadilly Circus loop, as she had reckoned she would.

She sat on a tree stump, let her head droop. She needed Steve desperately to comfort and advise her, and he wasn't there—this was her desolation. But even now, sunk in the depths of weariness and pain, she found the same core of strength she had discovered earlier and she hugged it to her. Her right leg was wet, Joey's jeans stuck to it painfully, and his sock squooshed unpleasantly in his sneaker. "Sorry about that, Joey," she muttered, knowing that her new strength wouldn't let her bleed to death, just as it would carry her through the defenses around Cotton Savage to uncover the last murderous secret. When she finally stood up, it was a feeling of invincibility. . . and pain. The leg was tightening up.

She had no idea what time it was. Somewhere in her flight she had lost her watch. Her bag of possessions were missing, too. Her mind fumbled to remember where she had left it, concluded it was in the thicket behind the Keller house. It didn't matter; all of her disguises were known to the police, except Gemma's wig, and good riddance to that. The burned-out house was still ten blocks away, half a mile, and she was limping. The backyard route was now impossible, and the shoreline too chancy; she decided to go by way of front yards, in order to stay off the sidewalks as much as possible.

Slow going. She crept up Piccadilly to Dover and over to Kings Road, which ran the crest of the peninsula parallel to Savage Road, joining it near the northern tip. Too often she had to dart onto the sidewalk to get around bordering walls and hedges and ornamental trees. At one house a barking dog woke someone on the second floor, a light went on, freezing her for an instant on the open lawn before she could hobble out of sight. Most of the houses were fast asleep, however, and she concentrated on putting one foot in front of the other.

Kings Road, six more blocks to go. The house on the corner of Albemarle was lighted. She crouched by a tree and studied it; only a troubled house would be awake. She figured it out. Boomer Smith's. As she watched, the door opened, someone came out, and the door closed again. She was momentarily blinded. The quickly glimpsed silhouette, large and shapeless, said it was Cousin Charles. She lost him in the darkness, frantically looked for him, then saw him at the corner, walking up Kings Road ahead of her. She stayed in her hiding place until he was out of sight. She waited five more minutes, watched a police car go quietly by toward Dover, then darted across the street to continue her laborious trek to shelter. The leg was getting worse.

Fifteen minutes of painful running and crouching and limping brought her to the corner of Brighton, a block before the Greystone Road, two blocks before Canterbury, where she would turn left to the burned-out house. A giant beech tree blotted out the street-light. At this point, a rock garden forced her onto the sidewalk, but she felt safe in the tree's umbrella of darkness.

Suddenly, arms reached out from the trunk, wrapped themselves around her, squeezed the breath out of her, raised her off the ground, squeezing tighter. She made squawking noises until her consciousness dimmed. Just as suddenly as she had been snatched up, she was roughly lowered and slammed against the tree trunk; a hand pushing against her chest kept her from falling. "You're as slippery as a snake, aren't you?" a voice said. She made out the blurry face of Cousin Charles close to hers. It didn't look at all sinister; actually, its glow of triumph gave it a rather jolly aspect.

Unable to talk, she could only stare at him.

"Yes," he said. "I saw you at Cousin Boomer's. The orange in the jacket stood out like a lighted match. I knew it was you." Strangely, the self-congratulatory tone forced an involuntary smile from her.

"Why are you doing this to me?" she whispered.

"You're a carrier of death, Mrs. Cochran," he said. The bantering tone was at odds with the words; the smell of whiskey was strong. "You're a plague that I intend to keep away from my family. Since the police can't seem to stop you, I'll just have to stamp you out myself." His smile seemed a happy one, though he pushed harder against her chest.

Creepy, she thought; but a rising anger, nurtured by a remaining shred of invincibility, nudged aside the horror. "Why did you kill my husband?" she demanded to know. "What did he ever do to you?" She squirmed against the restraining hand.

"Stephen Cochran?" he said lightly, as if playing in a musical comedy. "I didn't kill Stephen Cochran. He was doomed from birth when he killed Aunt Edith." He laughed. "She called him 'the accursed fruit of adultery.' He escaped his ordained death for thirty years, then you killed him when you brought him here. It was you, Mrs. Cochran." He laughed again.

"That's nonsense," she said. "Now I suppose you're going to say I killed Tish Smith, too, by casting a spell on her. I'm a witch."

"It's not a joking matter, Little Sally," he said. "You caused her death by escaping. I tried to help the police recapture you before you brought death to more people on Savage Point. As you can see, I was too late."

The man was sick and dangerous, but morbid curiosity caused her to ask one more question. "When you pushed her off the seawall, did you

think it was me you were pushing? Is that why you
did it?''

"Enough." Suddenly the bantering tone was
gone. "I will not dignify that with an answer. Will
you come with me quietly, Mrs. Cochran, or do
you want me to do something drastic here?"

"Where?" she asked. The hand was at the base
of her throat. Her last shred of invincibility fell
away, and she was thoroughly frightened.

"Greystone. We'll have a nice family council to
decide how to dispose of your case."

"Oh," she said as brightly as she could, "that's
very obliging of you. I've been wanting to talk to
your uncle. Thank you very much for inviting me,
Cousin Charles."

"Uncle Cotton won't be at this meeting," he
said. "And I'm not your Cousin Charles."

"Oh, yes, you are, cousin."

Her thoughts were hopping like a jar of fleas.
She doubted Charles had any intention of taking
her before a family council; more likely, he would
lead her to the seawall and throw her onto the
rocks. But even if he did convene a meeting of old
George Goldsboro, Nosy Alice, Virginia Goldsboro
and himself, it would be a kangaroo court with
four hanging judges on it. No, any stab at escape
had to be taken here.

The hand now moved to her windpipe. "Wait,
I'm coming peaceably," she said. Frantically she
weighed her next step. In her weakened condi-
tion, she was like a bird in his grasp. She could
never match strengths with him. His most vulnerable area was his huge stomach. Praying that her
wounded leg would carry her weight, she sudden-

ly brought the other knee up to her chest—forcing the hand to choke her for a fraction of a second—and kicked out, sinking her foot just below the solar plexus, knocking the air out of him. Her force and his recoil sent him away from her but only a few feet. She landed on her back, knocking the air out of herself, even as he was coming toward her again. She rolled twice, eluding his attempts to grab her, jumped to her feet and fell again as the bad leg gave way.

Come on, you miserable leg, she thought, unable to utter the words. She sprang to her feet, leaping sideways to evade his lunge. She ran, still without breath. Oh, Lord, how long can a body go without breathing? She gave a sobbing gasp and fell. Cousin Charles, lumbering after her, fell, too. It's almost funny, she thought, as she got to her feet and started running east on Brighton.

She ran downhill toward Harper Road, scarcely aware that the leg was functioning or that it had again started to bleed. At the corner she looked back and saw that Cousin Charles had stopped mid track and was standing there indecisively. She had no energy left to sneak through any more front yards or even to slow down to a walk. The running had a momentum of its own and, with luck, it would last until she reached her haven—provided someone or some force kept the police cars from Canterbury Lane for the next five minutes. Oh, Steve, if you're here, give me a lift and throw dirt in their faces.

Laboring painfully and sobbing out loud, she staggered across Savage Road to the forbidding hulk of a house, groped her way around to the

back, slumped to the ground with her back to the
basement wall. She lost consciousness for several
minutes, awoke with a start, unwilling to move. It
was fortunate, she mused quite irrelevantly, that
her pursuers were such a modern police force as
New York's and not an Alabama posse. Those old
boys would've just sat back and let the dogs do the
work. She'd've been run to ground long ago.

  She couldn't stay out here. Her body was stiffen-
ing all over. Somehow Willie Spencer had joined
Steve in her thoughts: Jesus, what a sad sack,
Willie Spencer was saying. Never you mind, she
shot back at him; I'm just resting here a moment,
that's all. Steve was saying, Sally, honey, get into
the basement. . . if you get into the basement, I'll
hold you in my arms and everything'll be all right.
You're on, she replied. Willie said, Me, too.
Dandy, she said.

She stirred, moved around the house in the
darkness, tried the basement windows, the
boarded-up first-floor windows, the two doors.
Nothing budged: Willie said, Break a window.
Steve said, No, the police might notice it. One
basement window had a little give to it. That one,
Steve said. She braced herself against the trunk of
a dogwood, and thrust her uninjured foot against
the frame. The second kick broke the latch with a
snapping sound, and the little window swung
open. She eased herself, feet first, through the
opening into the pitch blackness.

3

Sometime, early Tuesday morning. She was lying on cold cement. The pain filtered through her defenses—from the back of her head where it had hit the floor, from her rib cage that had cracked against something in her fall from the window, then the dull ache from her right leg. She seemed to remember she had been shot in that leg, a ridiculous thought; she tried to slither away from it, back into blackness, but her body was telling her with some urgency that she had to go to the bathroom. Oh, Lawdie! She opened her eyes a slit and a wave of dizziness came over her, followed by the first intimation of nausea. She clamped them closed and said, "Can't anybody do anything right around here?"

She opened her eyes, stared at the pipes overhead until the dizziness abated; she then turned her head to see for the first time the dimensions of her latest prison. It was an unfinished basement, cluttered at the front end near the furnace with charred beams and planking from the floor above. Gingerly turning to the rear, she saw an enclosed area near the back door that she prayed was a bathroom. She reached up, grabbed the edge of the workbench above her and pulled herself to her

feet, setting off clamoring protests from the injured
sites. As she steadied herself against the workbench, she noticed the small window above it and
realized she must have bashed her ribs against the
edge of the workbench after plunging through.
Silly place to put a workbench, she thought dazedly, right where people can crack their ribs against
it. She lurched toward the bathroom enclosure and,
a few seconds later, was sitting on the john with her
head over the sink, retching. Long after the spasms
had passed, she remained with her head against the
cold porcelain.

After a while, she sat up, feeling empty but
clearheaded. She saw that her hands were filthy.
She stood and peered into the cracked mirror over
the sink, rubbed some of the grime off it, saw a
big-eyed thing, The Creature from the Abandoned
Coal Mine. She turned the faucet; no water came
out. A shower head hung uselessly in a curtained
alcove. No water. An irrational horror gripped
her: she couldn't live another minute with all this
filth on her! She had to get water! Her mind told
her it had been turned off by the city after the
fire.

She tried to recall the cellar of their new home
on Dover, Steve leading her on a conducted tour,
earnestly explaining about switches, fuse boxes,
meters, gauges, turn-off valves. The turn-off
valve. The water could only be turned off inside the house, where it first enters from the
street. She hobbled toward the front of the house,
following the water pipes with her eyes, past the
hot-water heater, over a blackened beam and a
pick-up-sticks of partly burned planks, and there

it was, the round iron valve handle. She grasped it with both hands and turned. The shudder went through the whole house, and she turned some more. She heard the water coursing through the pipes, and she heard something else—water splashing freely somewhere above her. In panic, she hastened back, shutting off valves leading to the upper floors, standing on boxes where they were too high, until the splashing above her diminished and almost ceased.

Back in the bathroom, she turned on the water in the shower, jumped back when it sputtered, banged and spewed rusty brown water. When the water cleared, she got out of her clothes and boldly stepped under. The frigid water made her gasp, stung her leg; and for a moment the black fog threatened to come back. She held her face in the icy cascade; her hand found a sliver of soap in the tray, and she lathered herself until the soap disappeared. She turned off the water. No towel. Shivering, she flapped her arms, tried to brush the water off. She hated to put the dirty jeans and shirt back on, but she had no choice.

When she again looked at herself in the mirror, she saw a clean face with the drawn look of an Arctic explorer. She was cold. Worse, her dripping hair made her look like an undeniably certifiable loony. The only thing she could find to comb it with was a steel brush, which she doused thoroughly under the faucet before applying to her head, wincing. She tied her hair back with a piece of rusty wire. The wound had stopped bleeding. It was an elongated gash on the calf, not deep, with a large ugly bruise around it. She flexed her leg, and it hurt.

She had no idea of the time. She had put off thinking of the day ahead. Now the realization came to her that she had an appointment with a withered old man, from whom she would probably learn nothing: if she found the killer, she herself would be killed. She limped out of the bathroom and stopped breathing.

A male figure stood motionless just inside the window, backlighted by it so that his face was shadowed. "Steve?" she gasped. The figure took a step toward her and she saw that it wasn't a ghost or even a man.

"Hi," Joey DiGiorgio said, in a half whisper.

She slid down the wall of the bathroom enclosure until she sat on the floor. She pointed to him and tried unsuccessfully to speak. Something was crazy here. She was imagining things, seeing things that weren't there.

He glided toward her and she saw the pained look of concern on his face. "Gee, that's the thing I didn't want to do," he said. "I didn't want to scare you. I just stood there, thinking like maybe I should call out, and you came out before I could do anything." He reached down with his right hand. "Are you okay, Mrs. Cochran?"

"Oh, Joey, you scared me half silly," she said in an unsteady voice. "I never in the world expected—I thought I—oh, God!" She started to cry.

After a moment, Joey pulled her to her feet. "You have to get out of here," he said.

"I'm sorry. I don't think I'm in very good shape." She took the handkerchief he offered and wiped her eyes. "But what in heaven's name are you doing here? You couldn't possibly have known I was here."

"Well, not for sure," he said. "But I figured it out."

She shook her head in dull amazement. "You . . . figured it out?"

"It was only a guess," he said. "Either you were being hidden in someone's house, in which case I'd have been wrong, or you were hiding somewhere near the Savage house. I checked it out, and this was the only place. When I found the open window I figured I was probably right, so I came in."

"Why were you so sure I'd be near the Savage house?"

"Because I know you, Mrs. Cochran. I mean, I think I know you. The way I saw it, nothing was going to stop you from talking to the old guy. Then I heard on the radio that you got away from them at Mr. Harper's house, and that they searched another house and didn't find you there. I figured you'd run out of houses to hide in, that's all. It was just a lucky guess."

"What did they say about Barney Harper?" she asked.

"Nothing."

"They didn't arrest him or say they were holding him for questioning or something like that?"

"Not that I heard."

She let the tension drain out of her. "Joey, you really are something, you know that?" She touched his arm, and he flushed. "But why did you come? It wouldn't be good for you to be caught with me."

He stammered. "We—we thought you might need some help. And—and maybe something to

eat." He pulled a sandwich out of one pocket and
an orange drink out of the other. "It's only a sandwich. I told mom I couldn't put spaghetti in my
pocket." He half smiled at his joke.

"You're incredible," she said, uncomfortably
aware she had snatched the sandwich from his
hand. "You and that mother of yours."

"Eat it fast."

She mumbled through a mouthful, "You don't
have to tell—" She swallowed. "My stomach is
saying I haven't eaten in months." She took
another bite.

He looked down at the bloodied leg of her jeans.
"How's the leg?" he asked.

"They told about that?"

He nodded. "Shot in the leg."

She said, "It hurts, but it's nothing serious."

"Then I won't have to dig out the bullet?"

"Don't sound so disappointed."

He looked around the basement. "Nice place
you have here, Mrs. Cochran. Who's your deco-
rator?"

"Louie the Torch."

"Eat fast."

"I'm eating, I'm eating. What'd they say about
Tish Smith?"

"They just said it was like a funny coincidence.
Like, oh, by the way, there was another funny
death on Savage Point last night. They called it
bizarre." He fidgeted. "Finish up," he said.

"Why are you in such a rush to get me out of
here?"

He looked down at his feet. "Maybe the police
don't know about you wanting to see the old man,

maybe they do, I don't know. But, look, if I figured it out, they'll figure it out, too."

"They don't have your brains."

"Okay," he said in a monotone, "but there's somebody else who does know, and he can figure it out, too. The killer."

She stopped chewing and was once again aware that she was cold. The memory of Cousin Charles made her shudder. "What time is it?" she asked.

"Five after ten."

"Why aren't you at school?"

"I'm sick." He took his watch off his wrist and held it out to her.

She reached out to take it, then withdrew her hand. "Thank you, Joey. But time doesn't mean anything to me now. I'm going over there, you know." She nodded her head toward Greystone.

"I know."

"And it wouldn't do any good, you going along with me."

"Why not?"

She sighed. "For a lot of reasons, but mostly because I don't want you to get killed." He glowered.

"Now, look, Joey," she said, her voice rising. "It's *my* fight, not yours. I'm the fugitive, not you. I'm already in trouble, you're not. If they catch me, I'm no worse off. If they catch *you* with me, then you're in trouble, too. There's enough trouble in your family right now, so don't add to your mother's woes. So butt out, Joey Dee!" She poked him in the chest with her finger. "And that's that!"

He was shaking his head and frowning. "You

know what? You're something, too. You really
are.''

"Thank you," she said. "And thank you for the
breakfast. Now go.''

"We'll go together.''

"No.''

He shifted from one foot to the other. "Okay,
Mrs. Cochran, if that's the way you want it. Is
there anything else I can get you?''

"Oh, Joey,'' she said, and she hugged him.
"You're—you're just impossible. I'll see you soon.
I promise.''

He handed her the wristwatch. "Here. Now
you'll have to see me again. To give it back." He
went to the window, looked back at her. "Good
luck," he said. "Give the old bastard my regards.''

She said, "Joey!'' imitating his mother's routine-
ly shocked voice.

He smiled, and went up and out the window.

SHE STOOD AT THE BACK DOOR, studying the Dantine house through the skimpy hedge, wondering
why the yard seemed so strange to her. It was
empty. There wasn't a toy in sight, no bicycle,
rocking horse, ball, bat or racket, nothing to indicate there were young children in the house; nor
were there any rakes or mowers or other suburban
garden gear; just bare, straggly lawn and timid
bushes. The overcast sky of yesterday looked
more sullen, as if finally building itself up to a
rage. She lingered a moment longer to compose
herself, only to find her tension mounting and her
breathing turning to panting. She unlatched the
door, stepped out, closed it, and immediately

ducked down out of sight in the shallow stairwell.

Boomer Smith and Pastor John had come out of the house next door. "Well, thanks, Pastor," Boomer was saying. "All I want is something quiet and dignified. She was a good woman."

"A fine Christian woman."

"Nothing phony about her."

"A true daughter of Christ."

"Never mean, never for an instant."

"Full of charity and love for everyone."

"A temperate person in everything she did."

"The soul of moderation."

"Good wife and mother."

"Of course. What a terrible tragedy for you and the children and all the good people of Savage Point. Walter Keller will lead the choir, and Virginia Goldsboro will be at the organ. Good friends can be a great comfort at a time like this."

"Er, Pastor, I don't want to impose on Virginia. See if you can get another organist to fill in."

"She'll insist, I'm afraid."

"All right, but, for God's sake, don't let her sing."

"Not a note."

"Tish always liked the beatitudes. Maybe you can recite them at the service. They sort of fit—for theirs is the kingdom of heaven—don't you think?"

"Yes, she who was meek shall inherit the earth, and she that hungered and thirsted after righteousness shall be filled."

"Well, think about it. Maybe you better not drag in the beatitudes."

Sally raised her eyes over the edge of the stair-

well. Boomer, usually a sporty dresser, was en-
cased in a dark blue suit that was too small for
him; Pastor John was in his pulpit garb except for
the cassock. Grounded blackbirds in a desolate
scene. The clergyman said something she didn't
get, and Boomer said, with a sigh, "Leave her to
the police, John, just leave her to the police. I
know what your thinking is, so let's let it go at
that. I'm inclined to think she's just a scared rab-
bit, but what do I know? I feel awful."

Pastor John put a hand on Boomer's shoulder.
"There's isn't a thing you can do today except get
in the way. Leave everything to us. Go home and
try to rest, or you'll wear yourself down and get
sick."

Boomer smiled tightly. "A case of physician heal
thyself, eh? You know, I just may prescribe a quart
of Tish's best booze. An excellent idea, Pastor."

"You're not serious."

"Don't worry about it, John. I have to check a
few things with my idiot cousin, then I'm going
home. Thanks for everything."

Sally watched as he shook the pastor's hand and
marched to the opening in the giant hedge leading
to Greystone, an opening made through the years
by people bent on good works and holy business.
Watching him move, she sensed the effort of a
tired man determined to ignore fatigue and
despair and "to keep up appearances."

The tall minister lingered a moment in the yard.
He was doing isometric exercises with his arms
raised and joined before him. She found him a
frighteningly contradictory man, a modern,
ultraurbane man of God who mingled with sinners

with the utmost equanimity, and yet had a wild, unpredictable streak of the witch-hunter in him— with herself targeted as the witch. She had no doubt that he would slay the witch if God's justice required it. . . .

As she crossed the Dantine backyard and passed through the hedge, the first gigantic drops of rain fell, almost as if Greystone had its own private rainstorm. A distant rumble of thunder, then the nearby sky was split by a brilliant flash and, a second later, a mountain-fall of thunder made the ground tremble. The smell of dirt filled her nostrils as she hobbled hastily to the illusory shelter of the overhang over the back entrance to the Savage house. Soaked through, she pushed open the door and found herself in a kitchen large enough to serve a fair-sized restaurant.

"Whew," she said, flicking water from her hands. A tumble of thunder made pans rattle and, for a second, shut off her senses.

"Whew yourself," said a woman's voice.

Sally was beyond being startled by anything; her receptors were tranquilized, transmitting messages without coming near the alarm button, producing a serenity like that sought by Eastern cultists.

The woman was standing by the double sink, resting her buttocks against it, arms folded across her chest, gazing at Sally with cool interest. "Stand on the mat till you stop dripping, if you'd be so kind," she said. She was a large woman, thick and muscular like a wrestler, with untidy, graying blond hair, a broad peasant face and the soft accents of Ireland. Her white uniform was soiled at the thighs, where she was apparently in the habit of wiping her hands. Sally judged her to be about fifty.

Sally said, with all the dignity she could muster, "I'm Mrs. Stephen Cochran. I have an eleven o'clock appointment with Mr. James Cotton Savage."

"And I'm Mr. Savage's receptionist. Molly Allgood's my name." Her tone was good-humored, the face noncommittal. "May I ask the nature of your business with Mr. Savage?"

"I'm his daughter-in-law come to pay him a visit. Now if you will please—"

The woman pushed her rear away from the sink. "You appear to've stopped dripping," she said. "Come over and sit yourself, while we have a little chat." She indicated a chair alongside the kitchen table.

Sally said, "I'm afraid I—"

The woman said, in level tones, "You see, in addition to being his receptionist, I'm what you might call his faithful bulldog. It's my bounden duty to see that no harm comes to him. I'm simply wishing to ascertain your intentions, that's all, Mrs. Cochran."

"In that case, Mrs. Allgood—"

"Miss."

"Miss Allgood, I'll be delighted to tell you what you want to know. But I have little time, I must tell you that." She limped to the chair and sat down.

"Is your leg all right?"

"It's fine."

"May I look at it?"

"No."

"In addition to being a receptionist and a bull-dog, I'm also something of a nurse. You might say I am doctor and nurse to Mr. Savage." She looked questioningly at Sally.

"Maybe later, thank you," Sally said. "Right now, time is pressing."

The big woman sat down across the table from her. "I've been wanting to meet you, Miss Sally, if I may call you that. I don't mind saying I've been rooting for you, but then I always root for the fox in a hunt. And it doesn't mean you're going to get to see the old man if you're going to upset him."

Sally said, "I don't know if I'll upset him or not. I don't intend to. I don't even know what I want to say to him. I just know the answer to my husband's murder is in this house. And if his son's death is upsetting to him, I can't help it." She gazed earnestly, serenely, at the master's bulldog across from her. "Nobody is going to stop me from seeing him."

Their eyes locked in mild combat until Molly Allgood said quietly, "I guess you've earned the right, Mrs. Cochran. And it'll be up to himself to survive the confrontation with his past as best he can. He brought it on himself, the old devil, and I'm not of a mind to protect him from it. In fact, there's a part of me that wants to be there to see how he takes it."

Sally's brows went up in surprise.

"Don't worry, I don't propose to stay. Or even listen at the door. I don't do things like that. But I've been curious about this woman who caused all the trouble. She must've been something, to

knock a man like Cotton Savage off his feet. I
came about a year after she left. I've always been,
I'm admitting it, a little bit jealous of the woman
whose name he whispered. *Betty.* That would be
your mother-in-law, wouldn't it?'' Sally fidgeted,
and the woman said, ''What sort of a person is she
now?''

Sally searched helplessly for an answer. What
sort of a woman is Bess Cochran, when the more
urgent question was what sort of a man is Cotton
Savage. Trying to hide her exasperation, she said,
''A good person who doesn't really exist in the
present. She's a soap-opera character. I suspect
she sometimes whispers his name at night, too.
Okay?''

The bulky woman looked down at her lap.
''Thank you. I'm glad she's been true to him. Too
bad they had to keep on living. The end of great
romance should be death, don't you think?''

Sally raised her eyes, looking for the kitchen
clock. 11:05. ''I think he may be waiting for me,''
she said.

The woman's eyes were wet. ''She was beautiful, wasn't she, and he was so dashing. Oh, he was
handsome, he was. Makes it all wonderfully sad,
doesn't it? And here I was, just a plain old lummox
with a face that'd crack a mirror. But you don't
want to hear about that.'' She looked up at the
clock. ''I think he may be waiting for you,'' she
said, shifting to get up.

''Wait,'' Sally said. She shoved her speculations
regarding this sentimental amazon to the back of
her mind; there was a fascinating story there, she
was sure, but it wasn't the story she was after.

Sally reached across the table, put her hand on the woman's arm. "Maybe you can help me," she said. "Someone in this house killed my husband and tried to kill me, but I don't know who." Molly Allgood stared at her blankly. "Please, Miss Allgood, who'd want to kill Mr. Savage's son to keep him from meeting his father? Or, more likely, to keep the old man from meeting his son?"

Molly Allgood rose to her feet. "I think it's time to go up."

Sally said, "You love Mr. Savage, don't you?" She saw the woman's body stiffen, her eyes narrow. Sally said quickly, "One of these people committed murder—not to help the old man or to protect him or anything like that, but to harm him, to prevent him from seeing his only son, his only *child*, after thirty years. Don't you think it was a terrible thing to do to Mr. Savage? Wouldn't you like to find out who did it?" Sally's sense of detachment was slipping.

The woman remained standing. "They say you're insane, Miss Sally," she said slowly. "And surely it's a crazy idea you're saying, that one of them is a murderer. But if it's at all possible—" She nodded her head.

"Cousin Charles?" Sally suggested.

After a moment of thought, the woman nodded again. "If he stayed sober long enough, which he wouldn't. When he's in his cups, which blessedly is most of the time, he's a very humorous man. That's why I keep the bar well stocked with whiskey. But when he's sober, he's capable of anything. He can be very cruel, but I sort of forgive him. He's only a toady and he knows it.

The whiskey helps him forget it, puts him at peace
with himself.... No, this is crazy. I've been with
these people for thirty years and I just can't see
any of them doing what you said.''

Sally said, ''Virginia Goldsboro?''

''Possessive, strong-willed,'' the woman said.
''But you have to remember she was the apple of
her uncle's eye when she was a child. I can't say
she's still his little darling, there's a coldness now,
but I'm sure they must still have feeling for each
other. No, as I say, none of them would dare do
anything to anger him. He has the money, don't
you see?''

''Old George?''

Mollie Allgood waved her hand contemptuously.
''He hasn't the gumption to talk back to his wife.
You should hear her when she gets on him sometimes. He stands himself up straight like a broom
handle and sweeps out of the room.''

''How *about* Nosy Alice?''

''Who? Oh. Now that one has a mind of her own,
but she's very close to her brother. She's his other
bulldog, very protective. I don't think she could
lift a shotgun.''

Sally sighed. ''You're right, none of them
could've done it. Except that one of them did.
Unless it was an outsider close to the family, like
Walter Keller or Boomer Smith.''

''Why don't you ask them?'' the woman said. ''I
think they're still here.'' Sally looked at her in surprise. ''Don't look at me. I didn't invite them.''

No matter. She said, ''What do you suppose Mr.
Keller's doing here?''

''I don't know, Miss Sally. He doesn't tell me his

business and I don't tell him mine. To him, I'm just a piece of furniture. Overstuffed, you might say. It's a satisfying sight, if you don't mind my saying so, to see him jump when Mr. Savage tells him to jump. The old man scares him half to death. It must be terrible to live in fear that way." Her faint smile showed no trace of sympathy.

"Then why would he come here?"

"Whenever anything happens on Savage Point, they come here to get their orders, it's that simple." She went to a wall phone.

"I don't think I like the old bully."

Molly Allgood said, "He's not really a cruel man, honey. But if a toady comes to you and says kick me in the pants, wouldn't you be tempted to let him have it?" Sally half smiled at the thought of applying her foot to the broad beam of Boomer. The woman said into the phone, "She's here."

"Who was that?" Sally asked.

"Your escort service," the woman said.

Excitement suddenly welled in Sally, and she asked, "What does Mr. Savage know about Steve and me?"

"That's hard to say," the big woman replied. "I don't think he knew his son was living here until Sunday when he heard about the murder. He never used to listen to the news, but for the last two days he and I've been following your, what shall I call them, *gyrations* on radio and television. When you're not on the news, he seems depressed. Then you come back on leading them a merry chase, and he shuts me up while he listens."

Virginia Goldsboro was at the doorway. "Yes,

he's very interested in you, Sally. Come, he's looking forward to meeting you." She stepped toward Sally, her hand out in invitation. Draped in a light blue dress of silken material and with her hair sedately set in soft waves, she appeared more womanly than Sally had ever seen her; the only trace of her usually tailored look was the belt that matched the dress. She peered at Sally with concerned eyes.

Sally felt like a little girl who has been bidden by the nice teacher to come with her to the principal's office. It couldn't be bad because the teacher was smiling, although Sally vaguely remembered that the teacher, not the principal, had been the frightening one. She moved forward and let the arm encircle her shoulder. It gave her a sense of being protected.

A small hallway led to the formal entry hall, which had arched openings on either side; to the right was the darkened dining room, and to the left, the cavernous room that, to the young and starry-eyed Bess Cochran, had been nothing less than a "ballroom." It was dark and shadowed. Behind them in the entry hall and soaring above them was the elegant, semicircular staircase to the upper floors.

Virginia paused at the entryway to the ballroom. "We used to do our entertaining here," she said, her eyes glistening. "Would you believe sixty people dressed in gay summer finery, dancing to one of Lester Lanin's orchestras, and the tall, distinguished-looking host twirling and whirling the ladies till they felt light as butterflies? Even me. Look at it now. Haunted."

"Steve's mother called it a ballroom."

"That's what it was, in a way. Everybody having a ball. But you don't find a big country fireplace in a ballroom, not like this one. Can you see the sailfish over the mantel? That's been there from the beginning. Uncle Cotton caught it himself when he was a young man." A lightning flash lighted the room for most of three seconds. Sally saw the leaping fish and, beneath it, the shotgun. She shuddered.

"Oh, the shotgun," Virginia said. "Sorry, I'd forgotten about that. It was a present from my father to Uncle Cotton, and Cotton gave it to Cousin Charles because, he said, scattershot wasn't fair to the bird. He said hunting was a one-on-one contest, man against the bird, and if the man couldn't bring the bird down with one honest-to-God bullet—"

"Please, let's not talk about guns."

"Me and my big mouth. Well, you'll be happy to know that Uncle Cotton never did bring down a bird. I don't think he wanted to." She led Sally up the staircase. "I'm sure you've heard that Uncle Cotton is in a wheelchair."

"Yes."

"You may have difficulty understanding him when he talks. It's as if the tongue were just sitting there and not helping."

They stood before the solid wooden door to the suite of James Cotton Savage. Backstage. Virginia squeezed Sally's shoulder. "This is a big day for me, too," she said. "Your coming today is a godsend to me. We're going to be close partners from now on, right?"

"Right."

Virginia pushed open the door and said, "Gentlemen, she's here."

Sally's first impression was of the enormity of the room, which was directly over the ballroom and ran from the front of the house to the rear. The front, with its French doors and windows, seemed to be all glass. Except for the double bed smack in the middle of the room, the floor space was almost completely open; the sitting-room furniture grouping was set against the far wall near the front, across from the door. The most unusual feature of the room was the gymnastic equipment hanging from the ceiling, various rings and bars low enough to be used by a man in a wheelchair but now raised by tie-ropes and pulleys out of the way of ambulatory guests. Having glimpsed him racing his imprisoning vehicle on the front terrace, she could imagine the angry old man doing the same the length of the bedroom and raising himself on the swinging paraphernalia like a wild animal in a cage.

Walter Keller was on the sofa against the wall, Boomer Smith in a chair to his right, the figure of Cotton Savage, at the moment slumped forward, at Walter's left near the front window. All three stared at her without speaking.

Virginia pushed Sally toward the man in the wheelchair. "Uncle Cotton, this is Little Sally." The old man slowly straightened up, peered at Sally from the tunnels of his eye sockets. No expression showed on his face. Eyeing him from close-up, she saw the broad forehead and the too wide jaw that had seemed vaguely familiar when

viewed from the *Lord Jim*. They were Steve's.
The long nose was larger than it had appeared
through the binoculars, its prominence apparently
the result of erosion: the crumbling face had
receded from it, the mouth had sagged at a droll
tilt away from it, and the eyes had retreated
deeper into their burrows.

Virginia said, "Little Sally was the wife of the
man named Stephen Cochran who was killed the
other night, remember? They moved into the old
Wilson house next door to the Walter Kellers down
on Dover—" The fixed frown on the old face
deepened, and the good hand made an impatient
waving motion at Virginia, who said, "Me and my
big mouth again. I'll leave you two to get acquainted." She nodded to Walter and Boomer,
who half rose from their seats and settled back
again as Virginia left the room.

Sally stood before the wheelchair, looked calmly, at the old man. Walter Keller cleared his throat
as if about to speak, but Sally spoke first. "I've
been wanting to meet you."

The old man touched his chest, pointed to
her and said, "Me, you, too." The words came
out in low grunts, an ill-defined shorthand of
speech that he must have devised during his
decade of impairment as his best way of com-
municating. Thunder came from the east, more
faintly now, as the downpour beat against the
front windows.

"You're not very frightening, you know," she
said. "You look like an old pussycat."

The lopsided mouth tilted farther as the left side
tried to rise in a smile.

"You see?" she said. "You're really an old fraud."

"Now, Sally," Walter started to say.

The old man glanced at him and Walter subsided. He returned his attention to Sally, just as she tottered from a sudden wave of weakness. "Boomeh!" the old man said. Boomer jumped up, brought her a chair.

Sally said, "Thank you. It's just that I was ill this morning. I threw up." She looked gravely from one to the other. "And I never throw up. Never."

Boomer was studying her as if fascinated by her digestive woes.

Sally said to him, "Now, do you want to know what happened to your wife?"

Boomer's face shifted almost imperceptibly to a look of mesmerized horror. When she didn't speak, he nodded. She turned to the old man in the wheelchair, touched his arm lightly. "Forgive me, Mr. Cotton Savage, I don't mean to upset you, but this has something to do with why I'm here, and I really must say it." He waved a hand dismissing her concern. She turned to Walter Keller. "Did Henry tell you?" Walter's face had the same frozen look as Boomer's. He shook his head. "I think you're going to have to have a talk with him," she said. She turned to Boomer. "She was a very nice person, Boomer," she said. "I am deeply sorry to inform you she was murdered."

Boomer's voice was hoarse. "How do you know?"

"I was there."

"You were there!" Walter Keller exclaimed. "But, Sally, you couldn't have. You were—"

"Go on, little girl," Boomer said.

"That's right, Walter," she said. "I was with Henry. Dear Henry was being my gallant escort through the darkness. I don't know how much he'll remember, but it'll be enough to bear me out. Ask him." She turned back to Boomer. "We were making our way around the point below the sea-wall. We stopped to have a, let's call it, a discussion. Not far from here, you know the place, where the wall is about twelve feet high. We were close to the wall." In the simplest words, she told how the sudden loud whisper of her name caused her to respond, then the descent of the body from above, and again the loud whisper of her name in an inquiring tone. Boomer made her repeat some of the details. He questioned her again about Henry's rib injury.

Walter raised his hand to get attention. "Henry did say he slipped on a rock and hurt his ribs," he said. "That much of the story is true."

"Thank you, Walter," she said. To Boomer, she said, "Two murders. Steve and Tish. But were there two killers? I tried to consider all possibilities, including the possibility that you killed Tish."

"What made you think—" He was having difficulty talking; he swallowed several times.

"Only for a moment," she said. "Whoever killed Tish thought he was killing me. He called out my name. It couldn't have been you, because you are the one person above all others on Savage Point who would have recognized your wife in the darkness. You could never have been fooled into thinking it was me." Boomer nodded. She said, "I feel terrible about one thing. If I had stayed put, if I

weren't running from the police...she'd be
alive." Her emotions were real but somehow at a
remove, semidetached, dampered by a defense
mechanism against overload.

Boomer, looking down, breathing deeply, said
nothing.

Sally turned to Walter Keller, noticing he was
dressed in what she thought of as his "business
uniform," dark pinstripe, white shirt, dark tie. His
pink face bespoke petulance and bewilderment as
well as his usual eagerness to please. "What brings
you here today, Walter?" she asked.

"That's not important," he said. Sally's mind
raced off on a tangent, retrieved Mrs. DiGiorgio's
wig from wherever it was, and placed it on
Walter's head. Yes, the perfect barrister. Pom-
pous. He said, "What's more important is getting
this over with and getting you—"

Sally turned to Cotton Savage. "I think what
Walter's doing here is important, don't you?" The
old man, seemingly amused by her, nodded. "So
what are you doing here, Walter?" she said.

Walter's face got pinker. "I came to discuss
some legal matters with Mr. Savage that are really
none of your concern, Sally."

"It was about the will, wasn't it?"

Walter glanced at the old man, who nodded.
"Yes, it was about the will," he said, as if
begrudging the release of each word. "But we
hadn't gotten very far when Boomer came in. So I
can't tell you any more than that." He was obviously discomforted. Sally guessed he was
frightened, too.

She fixed Cotton Savage with a stare. "Would

you really fire Mr. Keller as your lawyer?" she asked. Walter sucked in his breath.

The old man started to say something, but, instead, propped a clipboard on his lap and wrote on it with an attached ball-point pen. He handed it to her. He had written, "You're a nervy one, aren't you?"

"Not really," she said to him. "What would *you* do if everybody wanted to put you in an insane asylum?"

He took the clipboard, and wrote, "They tried." Walter started to make popping noises.

Sally said, "Who?"

The old man waved his arm in an all-inclusive gesture. "Who'e fammy," he said.

"The whole family," Sally repeated. "Boomer and Walter, too?"

Walter said, "Here now!"

Boomer said, "This is too much!"

The old man glared at the two men, bobbed his head vigorously. "Fammy doccher, fammy hawyer, yeah," he said.

Walter sat on the edge of his seat. "Come on now, Cotton," he protested in a high voice. "You know I was on your side. I called in the neurologist."

Boomer stood up. "You're obviously in a bad mood this morning," he said. "You know doggone well I called in the psychiatrist who gave you a clean bill of health. And there was never any question of an insane asylum. I don't know what you're thinking of."

The old man kept bobbing his head, while an expression of something like glee came on his face.

"They didn't get away with it!" he wrote, and showed it to the three of them.

Boomer muttered, "Oh, for Christ's sake."

And Walter said, "You make it sound as though we tried to railroad you. We didn't."

Cotton Savage stared at them for a moment longer, then wrote, "True. Brought in honest doctors. Accepted honest findings. Hooray for you."

Sally said, "I think you're cruel. You've kept Walter in fear for ten years. I think you ought to tell him now. Would you ever take your law business away from him because of that?"

Cotton Savage glared at her, then looked at Walter. His face took on a sour look, as he shook his head slowly. Walter let out his breath and slumped back on the sofa. Sally said, "Thank the good man, Walter."

Walter said, "She didn't have to make you do that, Cotton. I knew it all along." He laughed nervously.

Boomer said, "I knew you were only pulling our legs. It wasn't very funny."

Sally said, "I'm sorry, everyone, for bringing that up. It really doesn't matter, except to Walter." She faltered. A distant flash of lightning brightened the front windows; she waited for the thunder that didn't come. "I really don't know what I'm saying. I'm just talking for the sake of talking, hoping I'll find out something that'll help me understand why Steve was murdered. I think maybe it's the will. You were going to change it, weren't you?" she said to the old man.

He shrugged.

"Thinking about it?"

He nodded.

"Whom were you going to disinherit? Certainly not your sister. Or were you?"

He frowned, held up his hand in a halting gesture, then he wrote: "Tell me about your husband. Where did he come from?"

Sally said, "Oh, he was your son, all right. He came from Mamaroneck and he was going to be a great lawyer. He was very good-looking." Her eyes were suddenly blurred, as she tried to study his face. "Yes, he looked something like you. He had your nose, only it wasn't as big. Someone killed him to keep him from meeting you." The few active muscles on his face moved haphazardly; she couldn't interpret their meaning. "They kept him from you as long as they could and, when they couldn't do that any longer, they killed him. Someone in this house. Someone in the will probably. I've been circling for three days, and now I'm here. Mr. Savage, whom were you going to cut out of your will?"

The old man's face set in a mask of wrath, and his hand shook. He bowed his head and remained silent. She was going too fast for him, she realized; he was temporarily turning off the influx of thoughts while he slowly settled in place the ones she had already thrust on him. After all, he was eighty-one and had been in virtual isolation for ten years.

Boomer said, "Well, I know he wasn't going to disinherit me, little girl, because I'm not in the will. I really have to go, Cotton. There's nothing for me to do about arrangements, but I have to be available just in case." He grabbed the old man's hand and shook it. "I guess I just came up to cry on your shoulder. It helped. Are you coming, Walter?"

As he started toward the door, he tapped Sally on the shoulder and nodded with his head for her to come with him. Walter Keller remained to assure Cotton Savage he could have a new will on a moment's notice. Sally went to the door with Boomer.

"I generally don't give free medical advice," he said in a low voice, "but have you given thought to the possibility that you're pregnant? I may be—" Suddenly he had to hold her up with his arm. "Easy does it, little girl. It's only a possibility. I'm probably all wet."

Sally blacked out for a few seconds in the doctor's arms. Somewhere deep inside her she must have known it. Her period had been overdue, seriously overdue, even before Steve's death. Something in her must have known. Steve's child! He hadn't left her, after all; he was still living. Her emotional lethargy vanished, and she felt transcendentally elated, suffused with grace. She felt holy.

"Why, glory be," she whispered. "I believe you're right, Doctor." She turned in his arms and kissed him.

He let her go abruptly. "I still don't approve of you," he said. "And I can't forgive you for Tish. It should've been you who was thrown off the wall, not her."

She said, "You may hate me, Boomer Smith, and I can't blame you, but I'm beginning to love you." She went to kiss him again, and he backed away.

"I need a drink," he said.

Walter joined them at the door, asked Sally in worried tones if she was all right. "Never better," she said blithely, and she kissed him. He backed away, more in surprise than distaste.

"Can I help?" he asked.

"Don't worry, Walter. Everything's going to be all right."

Boomer scowled at her. "I think you're wrong about, well, this murder thing, but if you find out anything—"

"I certainly will," she said.

After they left, she limped back to the old man in the wheelchair. *Everything's going to be all right now;* the old line circled her mind like a stuck record and she imagined she heard the background music swelling, but it was only the distant roll of thunder. Cotton Savage was wheeling about willy-nilly, scowling. His one good hand slipped on the wheel and he almost fell out of the chair. "Whoa," Sally said. "That horse is liable to throw you." She slumped onto the sofa and looked at him beatifically.

Twice he looked down at his hands and up at her, then he wrote, "Tell me about her." He added the name, "Betty."

Suddenly she was telling him everything she knew about Steve and his mother and fabricating details she thought would please her listener: Bess was still a lovely creature with silver gray hair, almost a recluse but very serene, active in charity work and much loved by the poor people of Mamaroneck. She failed to add that there were few poor people in Mamaroneck.

He nodded his head many times in approval. If he suspected she was exaggerating, he didn't show it. He started to write, looked at her in embarrassment, then finished his sentence. "Did she speak of me?"

"She never told Steve about his true father," she said. "That was the way you wanted it, wasn't it?"

He wrote, "I was a fool." He wrote, "A goddamned pussyfooting fool."

Sally nodded. "I think you were, but who am I to say?" He looked at her expectantly, awaiting more. Sally said, "I made her tell me about it yesterday. It must have been something rare that most people never experience. She's still in love with you."

He squirmed in his chair, turned it and propelled himself to the French doors where he faced the steady rain outside. Currents crackled noiselessly in the room, impelling her to rise from the sofa and move around, despite her aches. She paused behind him, peered out at the bay. The *Lord Jim* was barely visible, an impressionistic outline against a backdrop of gray mist. She said in a soft voice, "Betty remembered telling you it was 'yar,' not knowing what the word meant, just that it was something complimentary to say about a boat." The old man didn't move. Restlessly she walked to the rear of the long room, feeling she was wasting time she couldn't afford to waste, yet reluctant to press ahead. She peered out the back windows at the Dantine house. Modest cotton curtains in the second-floor window. No one there. She said, "I think Bess—I think Betty is going to be a grandmother." She turned to face him across the length of the room. He remained facing the bay. Did Sally imagine he sat taller in his chair? She retraced her steps toward him. "I'm not sure," she said, "but how does Stephen Savage Cochran sound to you?"

"Sounds very strange," said the woman in the doorway. Alice Goldsboro wore a tan cardigan over a silk print dress. She had a quizzical look on her face. "It has rhythm and a touch of alliteration, but that wasn't his middle name, was it? What's it all about?" She entered, wielding her cane as a stage prop as well as an aid. "Or am I being Nosy Alice again?"

"Oh," Sally said, "I was just playing a silly name game. Were you ever called Goldie by the kids in school?" She gazed coldly at the intruder who had broken the almost silent communication between her and the old man. But Alice, either insensitive to the vibrations or arrogantly disregarding them, proceeded to the sofa and lowered herself into it.

"I like word games," Alice said. "Cotton, I'm here. Come say good-morning to your sister. What a beastly day. What does that say on the back of your jacket, child?"

Cotton slowly turned toward her, no longer riding tall. He rolled toward her, gave her a peck on the cheek, and backed off. "Come back hater, sissy," he said. "Privack halk."

"Nonsense, dear brother, you know I can't resist private talks. Go on with what you were talking about and make believe I'm not here. It wasn't really a word game, was it?"

Sally said, "We were just getting acquainted, Mrs. Goldsboro. I'm new to Savage Point, and I was saying how much I liked it but how different it was from other communities. I was wondering why." She scarcely knew what she was blathering, loath to talk to this bumptious woman about anything so personal as the child in her womb.

"You weren't talking about that at all," the woman said. "But I'll go along with you. Savage Point is different because it was practically created by one man, the gentleman sitting to my left, my brother. And I'm quite proud of what he has wrought."

Sally, who had remained standing, turned to the old man. "Are you proud of what you have wrought, Mr. Savage?"

Cotton Savage glanced at her obliquely, looked quickly away. With agitated movements, he searched for and found his clipboard. He stared down at it for a long time, while Alice said, "Of course, he is." Cotton darted a look at her, then wrote, "I was." The clipboard remained in his lap, and the two women had to crane to see what he had written.

"Certainly," his sister said. "You had every right to be. And don't be coy with us, Cotton. You still are."

The old man stared down at the paper as if it were something horrifying, wrote again, "Created an evil thing. A monster. Killed my son."

Alice said, "My, aren't we depressed this morning. That's bushwa, Cotton dear, utter hooey. The truth is, I'm afraid, that Little Sally killed your son. Tell him, Sally." Her air was one of complete confidence that Sally would comply.

Sally ignored her. "Funny, that's what Steve's

mother said." The old man nodded in agreement. "But you're both wrong," Sally said. "I've thought about it a lot the last couple of days. Savage Point is a perfectly lovely area, one of the nicest in New York City. But people are people, and Savage Point somehow brings out an infuriating degree of smugness in them. There are worse sins than that. As your sister says, you have every right to be proud. So—" She touched him on the shoulder, and moved away from him.

Alice Goldsboro laughed. "You're a very clever person, my child," she said. "Cleverer than I thought. We used to call it buttering up. What do they call it now? A snow job. That was a perfectly marvelous snow job. I take my hat off to you."

"As one expert to another, Mrs. Goldsboro?" Sally said, restlessly roving, becoming fascinated by the gym equipment. Nosy Alice was making some sort of a retort, seemingly even-tempered, which Sally didn't hear. Running her fingers along the tie-rope that held one of the rings overhead, she noted that it was fastened by a simple slipknot to a hook on the wall not more than four feet above the floor, apparently so that it could be easily loosed by a man in a wheelchair. "These interest me, Mr. Savage," she said. "I'd love to see you use them sometime."

He made a sound that startled her until she realized it was a laugh. "Hike a monkey!" he called to her, and made the sound again.

"It's kept you alive, I should imagine," Sally said. "You have a strong instinct for self-preservation." She added, "Like me." The lethargy was sweeping over her again. The room, against all logic, gave her a sense of safety, even while her nerves were forcing her to keep moving. She started to pull the slipknot when a knock on the door interrupted her.

Virginia entered briskly, holding a silver tray with a glass of milk and a dish of Saltines on it. "Time for your midmorning fix," she announced to the old man. "Mother, I didn't know you were here." Strangely, to Sally, the big woman seemed disconcerted by her mother's presence. Sally noticed that Virginia was wearing her glasses.

Cotton Savage raised his head questioningly, and Virginia said, "I relieved the all-good Molly of the chore, because I wanted to make amends for irritating you, Uncle Cotton. I'm really a clumsy oaf, aren't I?" She moved toward the old man, noticed Sally lingering near the wall. "It's what the doctor ordered, a ration of warm milk spiked with a jigger of brandy, good for both body and soul. Here, Unc, drink up."

As she held out the tray to the old man, Nosy Alice reached out and snatched the glass of milk. "My stomach is rumbling," she said. "I think I'll just take this, and you get your Uncle Cotton another one, like a good girl."

Virginia said, "Mother, don't!"

The old woman raised the glass, silently saluted her daughter with it, put it to her lips with the air of a person who had had her own way all her life and couldn't conceivably change the pattern now. Virginia swung her hand and knocked the glass away from the old woman, spilling the milk on the sofa, the glass breaking on the hardwood floor. Nosy Alice looked up at her daughter with astonishment.

After a moment, Virginia stepped back, averted her eyes; the tray tilted, spilling the Saltines on the floor. Her mother said, "Well, I never!"

And Virginia said, "My! I did it again, didn't I?" She said, "I'm sorry, mother. That was the last of the brandy, and you know you're not supposed to have any alcohol. Now you spoiled my special peace offering to Uncle Cotton."

The old woman seemed to shrink into the sofa, a look of awful surprise on her face. "You mean it was *now*? I thought it was later."

Virginia said, "Mother, you're not making sense. I think you ought to go and rest."

The old woman said in an unsteady voice, "Yes. I don't want to be here." She struggled to rise, then sank back. Her plump cheeks were flushed red, her ancient mouth and the crumpled flesh around the eyes were a lifeless white. "Just give me a minute, darling," she said in a faint voice.

Virginia said, "I'll go and see if I can find more—" She looked at the old man in the wheel-chair, riding tall, with a stormy face. She looked at Sally, who stood with her mouth open. Virginia grimaced, spread her hands in a how-about-that gesture. "That tears it, doesn't it?" she said.

Sally moistened her mouth, managed to say, "What was in it?"

"Don't worry, it wasn't poison," Virginia said, with an amused smile. "Just a little old dissolved sleeping pill. I should've let you take it, mother, you'd have been fast asleep through it all. Oh, well, no use crying over spilled milk, to coin a phrase." She shrugged.

"That's not a phrase, it's a sentence," Sally said, while her mind grappled with dark thoughts.

"So I coined a sentence," Virginia said.

Her mother said, "Just give me a minute, darling."

Sally said, "You wanted to put Mr. Savage to sleep."

"Correct," Virginia said, looking owlish in her glasses. "I'm not really an unfeeling beast. I couldn't stand having him look at me. It would've been easier with him asleep."

"What would've been easier?" Sally asked, knowing the answer.

"Oh, come on, Cousin Sally," Virginia said. "You're smarter than that. How you ever connected us to the death of that bastard husband of yours I'll never know. But you did. That was too bad."

Suddenly, with a choked roar, Cotton Savage propelled himself at Virginia, who skipped back quickly to the door, saying, "No, I know how strong that arm is." She said over her shoulder, "Now, Charles."

Cousin Charles appeared in the doorway, looking confused. He carried the shotgun. Virginia took the gun from him and pointed it at the oncoming wheelchair. Cotton Savage stopped short. His face was a bluish red; he was breathing heavily. Whatever he was trying to say didn't come.

Virginia peered at him and there was concern in her voice when she said, "Calm down, uncle dear, it would spoil things if you had a heart attack. Oh, dear, I'm not very good at this sort of thing." Cotton backed away until his wheelchair bumped into the chair at the left of the sofa.

In a little more than a whisper, Sally said, "It wasn't Cousin Charles, after all. It was you, wasn't it?" She was leaning with her back to the wall.

Virginia flicked a glance at her. "Oh, Sally, you're still here. That's good."

Her mother moaned. "It's one of my attacks," she said in a feeble voice. "Virginia dear, have Charles help me out of here."

Charles made a move forward, but Virginia said, "No, I need you with me. Just close your eyes, mother."

Cotton Savage was staring at his sister, a thunderstricken look on his face. Nosy Alice started to whimper. "Oh, Cotton," she said. "I love you, Cotton," she said, and she started to cry.

Sally said, "It was you in our bedroom, wasn't it, Virginia?"

"Yes, it was, Sally, honey," Virginia said. "Would you believe me when I say I hated doing it?"

"Yes."

"Thank you for that."

"How did you get in?"

Virginia waggled the shotgun. "Move over here, cousin, so I don't have to keep looking sideways. This dear old man may take it in his head to charge at me again."

Sally said, "I like it here just fine. Besides, I don't believe I could move without falling down."

Virginia turned the gun toward her. "Don't be stubborn."

Sally said, "You wouldn't shoot me. The way I read it, it's not part of your plan. So please point that thing somewhere else."

Virginia sighed. "Have it your way. Makes no nevermind."

Charles said, "Shall I?"

Virginia said, "Leave the poor dear be. I think she's about to collapse." She swung the gun back toward the old man in the wheelchair. "Let's get this thing over with."

Sally said, "How'd you get in?"

Virginia wagged her head impatiently. "Oh, Sally, Sally," she said with another sigh. "I was the real-estate agent, remember? Real-estate agents have keys."

"So you knew who Steve was before we moved in?"

"Let's just say I thought it wise to keep a duplicate key. I didn't know what your husband was up to."

"But you suspected."

"Boomer suspected. He told me. Then I suspected, yes."

Sally said, "This is incredible. I thought one person was the killer, not a whole family! But where is the missing member? Where's your father?"

"Old George," Virginia said, in a tone of affectionate contempt. "Old George is the original Mr. Milquetoast. I expect he's up in his room cataloging his swamp flora or writing one of his gosh-awful poems, anywhere but here. If it weren't raining, I'm sure he'd be out on the meadow."

"Was he in on the murder of Steve?"

"Good heavens, no," Virginia said. "None of them were. That was my show alone. And if you...if you hadn't scurried away from the police, they'd never've known. You've made

things very difficult, my dear, but I forgive you.
Because everything's going to be all right now.
With your help.''

Nosy Alice said pleadingly, ''Charles?''

''Quiet, mother,'' Virginia said. ''Close your
eyes.'' She looked at her uncle. ''I don't suppose
you'd close your eyes for me, would you?'' The old
man, unblinking, stared at her. ''Oh, dear. Well,
what has to be has to be,'' she said, and raised the
shotgun. Alice whimpered.

Sally said, ''At Walter's party, he arranged to
introduce Steve to Mr. Savage the next day. What
I want to know is, did you make up your plan right
then? On the spur of the moment?''

Virginia's shoulders slumped. ''You are beginning to get on my nerves, Sally,'' she said. ''But,
no, I had the little old plan in the back of my mind
all along. Hoping I'd never have to use it, of
course.''

''Did you really believe—'' Sally pushed her
shoulders away from the wall. ''I'm beginning to
think you're the crazy one, Virginia. Did you really believe that your uncle would change his will
and leave everything to the son he never knew—''

''In a flash,'' Virginia said.

''—And leave all of you, his real family, out in
the cold?''

''You bet your boots he would,'' Virginia said.
''His *real* family! Sally, you sweet little innocent,
you have no idea what it's been like living here for
the past ten years. For the past thirty years, come
to think of it. This is a hell of a time to say it,
mother, but we never should've moved here in the
first place.''

Alice said, "No," in a muffled voice, whether in agreement or disagreement, Sally couldn't tell.

"Oh, it was all right for you," Virginia went on, apparently caught up in a flow of bitterness she couldn't quell. "You were his loving sister. But look at him now. Just look at him. What was it Charles heard Sally say that night? 'If looks could kill'? Look at his face now. We'd all be dead, including you, his sweet Alice. But for the rest of us it was a different story. We were the poor relations. Throw us a coin now and then, and we'd dance a jig for him. Well, the hell with that, Uncle Cotton! You've had your last dance!"

She frowned. "Okay, it's true, you liked me when I was a kid. You treated me like a boy. You always wanted a boy, didn't you? So I was your boy for a while and then you didn't like me any more and forced me to marry that strange young man from the firm, that...*child*, Al Summers. You made me fall in love with you and then you tossed me away to him like an unwanted toy. I guess that's what you did to that woman in Mamaroneck, too, but I don't feel sorry for her. Look at the look on him! You know, I'm glad I didn't put you to sleep, because I wouldn't't've been able to show Sally what the real James Cotton Savage is like."

Her mother said, "Virginia," in feeble protest.

"His *real* family," Virginia said, not hearing. "He looked on his real family with contempt, Sally, honey, and you bet your sweet life that if his bastard son had shown up, he'd have disinherited us like that, without blinking an eye. Well, I have news for him. Greystone is mine. It's where I belong. It's part of me, and of all the important things I've been able to do around here. And I'm not about to be tossed aside once again. Talk about Savage Point, I've done more for Savage Point than he ever did. It shouldn't even be called Savage Point. It should be called Goldsboro, that's what. Goldsboro!''

The gun was starting to shake in Virginia's hands. Cousin Charles said, ''Please don't change the name.''

Sally said, ''Why didn't you leave well-enough alone? As it turns out, there was nothing I could have learned from Mr. Savage that would have pointed to you as Steve's murderer.''

Virginia half turned to her. ''Sally dearest, please button your lip, or I'll have Charles button it for you,'' she said. ''It wasn't what *you* could've learned from *him*, but what *he* could've learned from *you*. He couldn't've proved it—nobody could've proved it— but he would've known. In fact, he already knew, didn't you, Uncle Cotton? That's why he wanted to talk to Walter this morning.''

The old man had said he created a monster, Sally thought, but he didn't realize the monster was his own niece. A bumbling, monomaniacal monster. Sally said, ''You aren't very good at this sort of thing, Cousin Virginia. For instance, why didn't you wear your glasses last night?''

Virginia said, ''That was stupid, wasn't it? I was so sure I'd see you sneaking along the seawall, I didn't think of anything else. For what it's worth, I'm terribly sorry about poor Tish. I'll have to make it up some way. But she had no business being there. In all the years she's been here, I've never seen her walk on the seawall. It's very dangerous for someone like her."

"And you were still acting alone?"

"Sorry to say."

"What made you bring the family into the act at this late date?" Sally asked in unfeigned wonderment. "Especially your mother. There was no way she was going to be disinherited. You wouldn't've cut off your sister, would you, Mr. Savage?"

The old man looked at his sister, and looked down. The old woman tried to lean forward and couldn't. She said, "Oh, Cotton, it's torn my heart out seeing you all crippled and shriveled like this. Sometimes I prayed for you to die, you've been so miserable. It's as much for you as it is for Virginia. Don't you see?" She sobbed. "Don't you see?"

"That's enough, Sally," Virginia commanded. "You're putting my mother through agony, and I won't stand for it. I'll just tell you this one thing, because I'd like Uncle Cotton to know it before he goes. You all seem to know the plan, but I'll say it anyway. It's simplicity itself. I brought my family in on it because I needed their cooperation, if to do nothing else, to stay out of my way.

"Sally, I said we were going to be close partners, and we are. We're together in this. I couldn't do it without you. First, I pull the trigger, and then you get the credit. Little Sally does it again. You see? Partners. Except the police won't know you had a partner, and they won't believe your ramblings about a family plot. That's appropriate, don't you think? Family plot. Sounds like a cemetery."

Virginia raised the gun to her shoulder and

sighted along the barrel at the old man's head. Her
breath suddenly rapid as if with mounting passion,
she said in a strained voice, "You lived too long,
damn you." Her mother closed her eyes and
moaned. Cotton stared at her fixedly.

Sally felt utterly powerless. The final act. Little
Sally does it again, and who would believe otherwise? Steve's child would be born in a sanitarium
somewhere. She whispered his name, but it was
Willie Spencer who answered, don't just stand
there, do something! Behind her back, almost as if
they had a will of their own, her hands completed
the pull on the slipknot holding the gymnastic
ring. It descended not quickly but slowly. She
screamed, "Virginia!"—anything to stay the trigger finger for a fraction of a second—and she
leaped for the ring with both hands.

Charles cried, "Watch it!" and the woman
started to turn.

The ring continued its downward swing, lower
than any trapeze Sally had ever been on. The tie-
rope, going through the small pulley on the ceiling, was holding it back. She raised her feet as her
rear touched the floor. Virginia was still turning
toward her; Charles moved to intercept her.

One swing, and it was taking an eternity. Her
feet, pointed with perfect Olympic form, slammed
into the woman's left shoulder, pushing her, spin-
ning her—and then the blast expelled all thoughts
from Sally's consciousness. She felt the recoil in
Virginia's body; the sound waves buffeted her. A
high scream stopped almost before it started, and
she wondered if it came from her. Her feet went
over Virginia's head, and her buttocks rammed the

woman's shoulder. On the return swing, her rear
end hit the floor and she let go of the ring, falling
heavily to the floor. For a moment she lay on her
back, with her eyes closed, listening to the protests of her ribs and legs. She opened her eyes,
raised herself to her left elbow.

Virginia, still holding the gun, was frozen in a
twisted position. Staring. Cousin Charles, behind
her and to her right, was staring. Sally followed
their gaze and saw the sight that had held them
rigid. The old woman sat propped on the sofa as
she had been since she had entered the room. She
would never be Nosy Alice again, for she had no
nose. No face. Blood spurted from the neck area
and, as Sally watched, the jet abated like a dying
fountain to a tiny flow, then an ooze. Cotton
Savage took one look, pulled his eyes away, lev-
eled them at his niece.

Virginia said, "Oh, God, mother." She straightened up and, in dazed tones, said, "She was here
only because I told her I needed her. I made her
choose between you and me, Uncle Cotton, and
she picked me. Charles, go see if you can stop that
blood, or she's liable to die."

Charles took three steps and stopped.

Virginia turned to Sally. "That—" She took deep
breaths in an obvious attempt to control herself.
"That was a terrible thing to do. Unforgivable!"
She swallowed. "It changes nothing, you know,"
she said more calmly. She touched the second barrel of the shotgun. "The shell in this gun isn't for
you, it's still for the old man in the wheelchair.
And you'll be charged with double murder." Her
eyes still fixed on Sally, she said to her cousin,

"Charles, never mind about mother, take care of
Sally here. No more tricks."

Charles stepped quickly away from the horror
on the sofa, and stood over Sally. Virginia swung
the gun toward the man in the wheelchair, aimed
it at his head. As her finger tightened on the trigger, she was suddenly in the embrace of strong
arms that wrapped around her from the rear. The
gun tilted up and discharged, blasting a hole in the
side wall clear through to the outside.

"It's over, Miss Virginia," Molly Allgood said,
grunting with the effort to hold the struggling
woman. "Just relax, Miss Virginia." She looked
over her captive's shoulder at Cotton Savage.
"Are you all right, sir?" she asked. But Cotton was
staring at Cousin Charles, who was now lumbering
toward the large servant woman.

"Kharles!" The command in the voice was
unmistakable. Charles halted one pace from the
grappling women. He half turned to face the
master he had known all his life. The old man
pointed imperiously at a spot alongside the wheelchair. "Come here!" he said. Charles looked at the
cousin he adored, now ceasing to struggle in the
arms of the master's loyal "bulldog." He looked at
his uncle. Indecision rooted him to the spot. Finally, Virginia was quiescent in Molly Allgood's arms,
and Charles moved slowly to his uncle's side. Like
a gigantic puppy heeling.

Sally lay on her back, looking at the ceiling. She
was in a strange gymnasium. She was conscious
but so removed from sensation that she might
have been in a coma. Later, strong, white-clad
arms lifted her and put her on Cotton's bed. She

heard other voices, men's voices. A blur of blue
uniforms. The police had finally caught up with
her.

One of the voices said, "And this one. Do I
understand she's some sort of relative?" Sally
waited for an answer, but none came. After a few
moments, she heard the same voice speak, as if
reading, "She's the mother of my grandchild."
Then, in a lower voice from farther away, "That's
a damn funny way of putting it."

Sally's hand fumbled at her jacket pocket.
Joey's watch. She must remember to give it back,
she thought. Her head rolled sideways, and she
was asleep.

Be a detective.
See if you can solve . . .

Raven House
MINUTE
MYSTERY #4

On the following page is Raven House
MINUTE MYSTERY #4, "A Sound Sleeper."

Every month each Raven House book will feature a
MINUTE MYSTERY, a unique little puzzler designed
to let *you* do the sleuthing!

U.S. (except Arizona) residents may check the answer
by calling **1-800-528-1404** anytime from March 1 to
May 15, 1982. U.S. residents may also obtain the solution
by writing anytime during or after this period to:

      Raven House MINUTE MYSTERY
      1440 South Priest Drive
      Tempe, AZ 85281

Canadian residents, please write to the following
address:

      Raven House MINUTE MYSTERY
      649 Ontario Street
      Stratford, Ontario N5A 6W2

A SOUND SLEEPER

Professor Fordney's attention was attracted by a suspicious-looking bulge in the right pocket of an obviously expensive camel's-hair overcoat, which was thrown carelessly over Skamp's green coat.

"That yours?" he asked John London.

"Yes, sir. You see...."

"Just a moment," interrupted the professor. A rather sheepish grin spread over his face when he found the bulge in the coat was made by a large peppermint candy cane. Examining the green coat, a sudden thought struck him. Perhaps that cane did have some significance!

He had already seen the body of Henry Skamp lying on the floor of the one-room apartment. Skamp had been stabbed.

"All right," Fordney nodded to London, "continue."

"Last night Henry came home a bit drunk, woke me up, and when I refused to listen to him tell about his love affair, he flung his coat on that chair and lay down beside me fully dressed. I was tired and went right back to sleep. When I awoke this morning—around nine o'clock—I found him lying there dead and called the police."

"You heard no sound after you went to sleep the second time, and you disturbed nothing?" the professor inquired.

"No—I was dead tired."

"How long have you two been roommates?"

"Oh, quite a while. About two years. I forgot to tell you that three months ago Henry lost his job and he's been brooding ever since."

"H'mm...." Fordney pondered a moment. "You're lying, London. I'm holding you on suspicion!"

How did the professor know London was lying?

From **Minute Mysteries** by Austin Ripley.
Copyright © 1949 by Opera Mundi, Paris.